# The Black Road

From the dark and brutal regime of Barkdale Penitentiary, Calvin Crow sets out to find and then kill the three men responsible for the death of his son, Walker.

Eventful and grisly, his journey leads him to Sego Bench, a booming silver mining town in Southern Arizona. There he slowly settles to a different life and the troubled nightmares of his past gradually fade as he builds new alliances and finds new friends.

But the peace is to be short-lived when Denton Lome then rides into town. He is the sadistic, bullying sheriff-elect, and a man with good reason to conceal his true identity from Calvin. When innocent miners get robbed and murdered, a confrontation between the two men becomes inevitable and lead is destined to fly.

# The Black Road

### CALEB RAND

**A Black Horse Western**

ROBERT HALE · LONDON

© Caleb Rand 2001
First published in Great Britain 2001

ISBN 0 7090 7022 5

Robert Hale Limited
Clerkenwell House
Clerkenwell Green
London EC1R 0HT

Typeset by
Derek Doyle & Associates, Liverpool.
Printed and bound in Great Britain by
Antony Rowe Limited, Wiltshire.

# 1
# On Track

It was nearing midnight and the train was south of the Edwards Plateau, rolling close to the Pecos River and Langtry.

In an empty box-car, Calvin Crow climbed wearily to his feet. His recurring nightmare had exhausted him and he trembled, his body griping at every movement. He stepped to the open gap and saw distant town lights, felt the biting slash of rain across his face. The wind gnawed, and he held a buff jerkin tight around his ribs. His left hand rubbed at his face, fingered the livid scar that marked his pale forehead. He turned away and groped for his bedroll, swung its tie-string across his shoulder. Then he waited, staring out into the rain-thrashed night.

Ten minutes later the train lurched and slowed, its approach whistle hooting against the squeal of braking wheels. Cal kneeled and gripped the rail of an iron-framed door, eased his body out of the car. He took a deep breath, then with his legs on the move he let go.

He felt the crunch of the ground, tried to retain his

balance. But his feet slipped and he fell in the gummy sludge beside the track. He was within inches of the train's wheels, but he lay there stunned. Then the roar and clatter quietened down and he saw the red lights of the caboose fading into the distance.

He lay still, listened to his rasping breath. The howl of the engine's whistle eddied back through the wind, then the only sound was the steady hiss of a winter rain.

Unsteadily he got to his feet, slick with mud and chilled to the bone. Then he stiffened when the glow of a camp-fire flared out of the night. For a moment he watched its shaky flame, then started towards it, shuffling some because of the fall.

The fire was burning in the lee of a trestle bridge that spanned the Pecos. He clambered down the sloping bank, awkwardly using his hands to steady himself. He heard the spate below him, saw crimson reflections in the white-churned water.

Outside the edge of the firelight he stopped, adjusted the string of his bedroll across his shoulders. He called out into the darkness.

'Hey there . . . I'm comin' in.'

He waited unmoving and silent, called again. Then a man's voice answered.

'You'd make a poor Injun, whoever you are. Step forward so's we can get a look at you.'

Cal limped forward, stood off from the fire. It was beyond its best, although protected from the rain by the dense criss-cross timbers of the bridge. On a rocky ledge that was half-buried in the mud of the bank, sat three men. They were indistinct figures, but Cal saw they were dressed rag-tag. They were bearded and their clothes were stained dark from rain and chafe.

Cal's pulse increased and he swallowed hard. But he'd been frustrated in his search too many times to believe that another group of jayhawks or hobos might be the ones he was searching for, knew enough to cover up his hunger for revenge.

One of the men looked up, squinted.

'We ain't got grub or coffee,' he said thickly. 'But you can sit by the fire if you've a mind.'

'Goddamn hell of a night.' The man sitting furthest away grunted, spat something into the fire. 'Yessir. It's a night for no good.'

The man in the middle said nothing. In the firelight, his straggly bearded face was hard-pinched and unmoving.

The first man spoke again. 'Hey pal, you ain't no Texas lawman, are you? A dangerous con, maybe?'

Cal shook his head.

'No,' he answered, 'I ain't either.'

Cal wasn't a Texas lawman, but he wasn't far from a dangerous con though, having spent three months in the Barkdale penitentiary. His son, Walker, had done time there too, as a prisoner of the Border Troop. But now he rested in an unnamed grave, a few discreet miles outside of the town.

Calvin and Walker Crow had both been innocent casualties of the clear up regime of the Border Troop. In the main, the "Troop" had been ex-army; amnestied deserters who were paid a bounty by the state legislature. Their mission was to patrol the Rio Grande from Laredo to Del Rio; clear the border of drifters and lawbreakers. Until they were disbanded by Washington, it was a task which they carried out indiscriminately and with sadistic, brutal fervour.

Cal ground his teeth, looked around for somewhere to sit. He grabbed at some withered smoke-thorn, tossed it on the fire. He kicked, tested a stump with his boot-heel and sat down. The man who was nearest started to cough gruesomely, and Cal turned his head away. The rain had strengthened and it began to drip on the fire. The sizzle and spit mesmerized him, and he started to doze, his head jerking backwards and forward on his chest.

When he woke, the fire was almost out and he pitched on the last of the damp brush. The meat train running east to San Antonio had just gone through, and some loose dirt splattered down from the overhead trestle. Wary and apprehensive, Cal looked up, tried to shake away the damp stiffness as a big, solid figure came slithering down the bank.

In the grey, pre-dawn light, the man who was clutching a slouch hat got to within twenty feet of the fire before he stopped. Water ran down his forehead, glistened on his dirty, stubbled face. He snorted, pushed a hefty fist against his nose and mouth before shambling forward a pace.

It was the nasal grunt that wrenched at Cal's stomach, the hand gesture that sent his blood racing. He knew the man instantly.

'Dillard Groff,' he rasped.

The heavy man paused uncertainly, until Cal's face came clear through the curtain of rain. Then, as some twigs hissed and spat from the fire, the man took a step back, his hand scrabbling at a fold in his sodden coat.

'I know you from somewhere?' he questioned, nervously.

Cal didn't move, he just stared. Only his eyes revealed the chilling hostility.

'You *did* know me, Groff,' he answered without feeling. 'You looked after me an' my kid at Barkdale. You even helped me bury him.'

Groff stood his ground, his mean features working on the memory. Then violently he drew the Dragoon Colt. Sharp flame burst from the gun's chamber and a .44 bullet slashed instantaneously through Cal's jerkin.

To the side and behind him, someone yelled. Without taking his eyes off Groff, Cal heard the other men breaking for cover among the wooden trestles of the bridge.

Groff fired again, but he was already backing away, unnerved and too shaky for an accurate shot.

Coolly, Cal's right hand moved, and first light glinted along the honed blade of the beaver-knife he pulled from the sleeve of his left forearm. He showed it to Groff and moved forward.

The Dragoon Colt blasted twice more, and Groff's feet dragged at the mud, as he turned to scramble up the slope of the river bank.

But Cal came on, any risk sided with single-mindedness.

'That's four, Groff. Two more misses an' you'll have to outrun the Pacific Flyer to get away from me,' he shouted.

Groff's response was another wasted shot that embedded itself deep in a wooden prop. Cal grinned severely, looked up. Through the rain he saw Groff outlined against the leaden sky, saw the big man lose his footing

9

as he tried to make the track. Cal followed, got to the top
as Groff started to run for the far side of the bridge.
Groff turned. He saw Cal closing and he grasped an
upright brace, swung away from the track. He kneeled,
tried to roll beneath the footings, but couldn't make it.
Cal stopped. He moved to the other side of the bridge
and, using the uprights as cover, got almost opposite
Groff.

They were less than twelve feet apart, and Groff
panicked, pulled the trigger for the last time. Cal swore
with relief as the bullet ricocheted from a big iron plate
to the left of his face.

'I make that six, Groff,' he said as he stepped out on
to the track. 'You've had more chances than you ever
gave anyone at Barkdale, you gutless scum.'

Groff hurled the big Colt at Cal, who flinched,
deflected it with his knife arm.

'Now you're done,' he yelled. 'No one to torment or
pole-beat, any more. No more sheriff's guns or state
bigwigs to protect you. Your life's over, Groff.'

Cal wondered whether he'd have the cold-blooded
stomach when the time came, but he did. Dillard Groff
was one of the Border Troopers he'd sworn to run down
and kill.

'You remember Walker Crow?' he asked the man who
was glaring back at him with scared, red-rimmed eyes.
'He was fourteen years old, Groff . . . never harmed a fly.
Remember you beat him until he was dead; lyin' broken
in the muck of the pen . . . his own blood? I can't get my
youngster back, Groff. All I can do is kill you . . . when
you've told me where the others have gone to ground.'

'I heard most of 'em are chilli-pickin' around Las

Cruces. I ain't goin' anywhere near 'em. What you goin' to do now?' Groff almost squealed in panic.

'I already told you.'

Groff couldn't bear being strung out. He roared his enragement, rushed across the track at Cal, who sidestepped, swung the big blade.

He thrust deep, headlong and low into Groff's belly. Up close, the men's eyes locked, but it was Groff who saw the black mist.

'You're goin' to let me go?' he asked, in curious, fatal despair.

Cal almost lost his footing on a wet sleeper as he twisted around. He held the blade deep in Groff's stomach. He slipped his other hand into the dying man's sticky vest, pulled a money-bag.

'Yeah,' he said simply. 'But I need a stake. Gotta get me to Las Cruces.'

He twisted the knife, jerked it free. Groff belched, reeled on the edge of the bridge. Then he pitched slowly forward, down into the rain filled obscurity of the Pecos.

'Go to hell, Boss Man,' Cal said, his heart thumping. For a short while he stood there looking into emptiness, then he pulled off his hat, lifted his face to the rain.

'It's only one of 'em, son,' he muttered, then turned away.

He'd sent Dillard Groff to meet his Maker, but he still had Crick Gibson and Jeeter Krewel to dispatch.

Cal felt the cold sweat break across his body. His gut spasmed and his hands started to shake. The fever was returning. With his nightmares, it was another wound Cal suffered from the Barkdale penitentiary.

He forced his thoughts to New Mexico, looked west

along the glistening track towards what would be the start of his journey.

# 2
# Big Change

There were four saloons, eight bars and maybe ten dog-holes in Las Cruces, and it took Calvin Crow most of three hours to visit them all. He passed unnoticed, didn't ask questions and tried not to make eye contact. When the sun finally dipped, he spent fifty cents at an end-of-town chuckwalla. He ate ribstick and drank his belly-wash coffee quick, before getting on his way.

At first he'd felt hopeful, even eager as he made his way through the town. But Gibson and Krewel weren't in Las Cruces. If they had been, he hadn't recognized them or was too late.

Sitting on a bench outside a hardware store, he tried to put faces to the two men. He'd never heard Crick Gibson say anything to anybody, but he'd seen him up close.

Cal had carried Walker to the guards' cabin at Barkdale the night he'd died, begged them to get the town doctor. But Gibson's consideration had extended to prodding the unconscious boy with the tip of his rifle and covering him with a damp horse-blanket. Cal

13

himself was fevered, but he remembered a big man with pale watery eyes who carried a Sharps carbine.

Jeeter Krewel was a lean, young tormentor, who had a bandoleer-style holster and a liking for pistol-whipping. But much of Cal's recollection on looks was now hazy, and any one of the cowmen or drifters he'd seen that day could have been a trooper or a guard at Barkdale.

Cal closed his eyes for a minute, forced out the memory of his son. It was Dillard Groff – one of the men who liked to be called 'Boss Man' – who'd beaten Walker to death. Over a period of weeks, he'd used a cow-pole; started on Walker's feet and legs, worked his way up.

Cal took a deep breath, clenched his fists with suppressed anger. Walker's guileless face emerged before him. Against the night sounds of Las Cruce's main street, he could still hear his boy's raw, pitiful cry. 'I'm cold. Don't let me die, Pa.' The words that gave him such tormented sleep.

The night wind whipped the street and he shivered uncontrollably, pulled his jerkin close. He thrust his hands into his pockets and felt the remaining money, swore resolutely. He eased himself from the bench and walked across the dark street to a workers' emporium.

Fifteen minutes later he was back on the boardwalk carrying two paper-wrapped parcels. He had a quick look up and down the street, then re-crossed between a skinners' train and an ore wagon. He went into the lit-up general merchant's store that he'd noticed had a barber's shop to the rear.

He sat in the cutter's chair and leaned back. He half-closed his eyes, read the price for a hair-cut, grinned at the cost of a bath – with or without soap.

'It'll be like shavin' a buffler chip,' he said, 'an' I'll be needin' a bath . . . with soap.'

'Ain't that the truth.' The barber smiled, spoke without considering offence. 'I'll get Fat to put on more hot water. Cost you a full dollar.'

Cal nodded.

'I've accounted for it,' he said, and settled back in the chair.

The barber shouted, and out of the corner of his eye Cal saw a small pigtailed figure push aside a modesty curtain.

Thirty minutes later Cal focused on the mirror facing him. For the first time in months he had a good look at himself, saw the hurt of terrible memories in his eyes. But his face was clean and the back of his neck felt stark and cool. He extricated a dollar from his pants pocket, matched it with another. It was late in the day, but the barber had taken his time. From the neck up, Cal thought he looked like a city greener.

'Tub's ready,' the barber said. 'You want that Fat should help?'

'Wouldn't wish that on anyone . . . not even John Chinaman,' Cal rumbled.

With his packages and his bedroll, Cal walked past the curtain. For the first time in many weeks, he undressed fully, dropped his rancid clothing on top of the bedroll.

As the Chinaman poured another pail of steaming water into the wooden tub, Cal indicated the clothes.

'Fat,' he said. 'There's a dollar, if you take those duds out back and set a match to 'em.'

'Yeah, dollar,' Fat chuckled and immediately disappeared with the filthy heap.

Cal stepped into the tub and lowered himself cautiously, made a few ooh and aah noises at the almost forgotten sensation of hot sudsy water.

The long day took its toll and Cal's eyelids felt heavy. As his eyes closed, he heard the Chinaman shuffle in and out. He could hear the barber telling a customer that the store was closing for the night. Then he tensed, opened his eyes when the talking stopped.

When the curtain swung away, a thin, dark-featured bearded man stepped into the wash-room. Cal recognized him straight off. It was one of the hobos from the trestle-bridge outside of Langtry; the one who'd offered him a seat by the fire. But now the man was wearing a store-bought suit. He studied Cal silently for a moment, then his eyes took in the small room. He shook his head, smiled thinly.

Cal guessed what he was thinking and smiled back. Gripping the knife, his right hand emerged from the tub. Water glistened and ran the length of the blade, dripped to the floor.

The man whistled through his teeth.

'Green River knife,' he said. 'Very fine, but it don't replace a big Colt.'

Cal continued with his smile, but colder.

'It ain't meant to, friend,' he replied. 'I've seen a man with half his bread basket shot away, live for five days.' His hand twitched. 'This ain't ever given anyone that kind o' trouble,' he added.

The man stared at Cal, read nothing in the spare features.

'You've a way about you feller,' he said thoughtfully, 'and there's an ugly son of a bitch still swimmin' in the

16

Pecos would swear to that.'

Cal laid the knife beside the tub.

'Get out o' here,' he said, not unfriendly.

The man shrugged, stood the other side of the curtain.

'Got in from El Paso a couple o' days ago,' he said. 'I'm goin' west . . . the Pacific maybe. This Las Cruces ain't too friendly a town after dark. A bunch o' cowwaddies are kicking the crap out o' Main Street.' A wary grin slipped across his face. 'They're all likker'd up an' the Sego Bench stage don't leave until midnight an' that's a long hour away. I saw a friendly face come in here.' The man laughed. 'I sure as hell wouldn't o' recognized you from away off.'

Cal unwrapped his parcels, dressed slow and satisfied.

'You an' your friends didn't look too prosperous neither, the last time I saw you,' he suggested.

'From what I recall, I told you we had no vittles. Never said anythin' about money. At the time, it didn't seem the wise thing to do.' The man stepped back into the washroom, held out his hand. 'I'm Franklin Henner,' he offered.

After pulling on his stovepipe boots, Cal buttoned the blue hickory shirt around his neck. The short capote was buttoned and fitted well.

'Calvin Crow,' he said. 'What else do you know about me?'

Henner eyed him with wry concern.

'A little. You're lookin' to settle up with Texas . . . some o' the Border Troop. From what I heard that night . . . can't say I blame you.'

Cal thought for a moment.

'Yeah. What else do you know?' he asked.

'I know there's some of 'em in town right now.'

Cal's body tightened. He cursed silently as he picked up the money, ran his thumb along the blade of the beaver-knife, thrust it into its arm sheath.

'But if you take 'em on without a gun, you'll be a permanent resident of Las Cruces, whether you like it or not,' Henner went on.

'What's that matter to you? Why'd you follow me here?' Cal demanded.

Henner wiped the back of his hand across his mouth.

'You got to be in support o' somethin'. For me it's the underdog.'

'How'd you pay your way, mister?' Cal asked, disgustedly.

'Knowin' where the safe money is . . . goin' with it.'

Cal pushed up close to Henner. So close he could smell the newness of the man's suit.

'You got any money on what happens when I leave here, gamblin' man? You reckon on makin' a few dollars with these troopers? You *goin'* with them?' he threatened.

Henner laughed nervously.

'A man has to make a livin'. Why not out o' those that hold life cheap . . . an' I'm talkin' about *them*, not you, Crow.'

'That don't make sense. You won't be makin' any money from that scum, an' your hopes of me rewardin' you are . . . well, just remember that *hope* makes for a poor supper.'

'If you think I'm bluffin', Crow, consider well. When it's your life . . . *that's* a big bet. You only lose it once.'

Cal moved to one side, stooped to take a quick look at himself in the mirror.

'Ready to face the big bad world, Dude?' he cavalierly asked his reflection.

Cal didn't doubt the company he'd be in when he took to the street. Henner wanted to bet on the outcome, not whether any murderous renegades were actually waiting.

Cal turned fast. His right hand swung up under Henner's chin and the needle-sharp point drew a trickle of blood.

'If I pushed hard enough . . . reckon I'd see it slide past an eyeball,' he said without emotion. 'Now, tell me their names . . . these mean gunnies.'

Henner swallowed hard.

'Bittleman . . . Waxy Bittleman. The other one's called Krewel, but he'll more'n likely run.'

Cal bridled at the mention of the name.

'What's he like . . . Krewel?'

'Skinny . . . mean eyes . . . wears a bandoleer.'

Cal swore, shoved Henner past the curtain.

'Let's go. You're runnin' point.'

The barber, who was sitting in his own chair, looked up. He was interested, but also worried. He'd guessed or heard what was coming.

Henner walked straight to the door, held up for a second. He turned his dark face to Cal.

'I'm goin' north. I can't think what the hell you're goin' to do without a piece, but you'd better do it quick.' He spat to the floor and swore loud, flung the door wide. Then he went through it, jumping to his right with the quickness of terror.

Cal followed him in one long leap. He heard a shout, saw movement at the edge of his vision. Henner hadn't been bluffing, nor were the men across the street. Guns flared in the darkness, and Bittleman and Krewel weren't drunken cowpokes.

# 3
# Out of Las Cruces

Cal wasn't of the panicking kind. Nevertheless, with his head low, he twisted south and ran fast.

Behind him, Krewel cursed, and the window of the store shattered, the lamp inside flaring for an instant before crashing to the floor.

Cal didn't stop, instead doubled back, turned north in the direction that Henner had gone. He heard another shout, then a single gunshot. The man who'd remained across the street was behind a water-barrel, crouching low and shooting. Further up the street, an empty stock-freighter came slowly towards him. He heard the driver shout at his oxen, then saw him jump from the seat, take avoiding action from the crossfire.

The freighter came on, and Cal ran to meet it. He stepped on the wheel-hub and vaulted into the bed of the wagon. Bullets crashed into the side panels and Cal hunkered down, the moonlight glinting blue on the Green River knife. He counted ten, then fifteen seconds, before smartly cartwheeling himself back to the street – alongside the water-barrel.

21

He saw Bittleman's waxlike features, saw the lurid flash as the gun exploded, felt the hot punch as the bullet tore past his face. Then his left hand was clutching at the man's throat. Both men went back against the low boardwalk, but Cal's knife was already being forced between the gunman's ribs.

Bittleman cried out, then gurgled. He dropped his revolver and his tough fingers clawed at Cal's hand. He spluttered blood and Cal turned away, mindful of his new coat.

The man sucked in his last air as Cal slowly pulled out the knife.

'Bet 'em high an' sleep on the streets,' he muttered. He looked to the freighter that had come to a halt in the middle of the street. The near side ox's head was turned towards him, its great bulging eyes shining in the dark. 'And what's your problem?' he added.

He peered into the empty darkness around him. Someone came running along the boardwalk opposite, and when they were level with the freighter they stopped, veered into the street. Cal thought of Krewel and swore, took a measured step back.

It was Franklin Henner. He was holding up his hand, breathing short and gasping. He stared at the man who lay face down in the dry, dark mud and shook his head.

'The trouble is, with a knife, there's no noise. You never know what it's doin'. It's very scary,' he said. Then he looked back at Cal. 'But I'm glad it's over. I got too many years for this kinda work.'

'I never noticed *you* workin', Henner. You said there were two of 'em layin' for me. Where's the other one . . . Krewel?' Cal asked, kneeling to wipe the long blade

22

across the gunman's arm.

'God only knows. I wasn't goin' to follow him.' Henner was still blowing hard. 'If you're travellin' light, Crow, now's the time to run. You've already done the cuttin'. We' must o' been seen, an' I don't intend to sweat out any time in some adobe rat house; not for what you done here tonight. The Sego stage leaves in half an hour. I suggest we be on it.'

Cal pushed his knife back in its sheath.

'You had this figured?' he asked quietly. 'For what I done here tonight? Goddammit Henner, there's no one in Las Cruces knows me. This is down to you. You mouthed off . . . gave some rawhider my name. That's when you made your bet about the outcome. That's why there's no one on the street, you louse.'

Henner went for a daring smile.

'Like I said before, a man's got to make a livin'. Rules an' etiquette's for Easterners. Come on, let's paint our tonsils. We deserve it.'

They went across the street and Cal heard some scurry and talk behind them. He looked back and the noise ceased. They took the steps on to the boardwalk, hesitated as a tall, heavy-set man brushed past them. Cal stared after him. Under weak lamplight, the man looked angry and purposeful.

'Lawman,' Henner said simply, before indicating Toffee Johns.

The saloon was thick and noisy; mostly good-natured miners and skinners, punchers from outlying ranches. Like Fat, the Chinaman, who was now sitting in a corner feeding crumbs to a caged bird, they paid little heed to the two men who jostled their way to the bar.

Cal was mindful of any interest he might attract because of his new outfit. But his new clothes had been calculated, a trade-off against looking anything like a down-at-heel or gunslinger, even.

Henner made it to the bar and used his elbows on the men either side, motioned Cal to get in beside him. He caught the barkeep's attention and two single-shot glasses were banged down in front of him. He poured the high-coloured whiskey into his own glass, waited for Cal to do the same.

'Here's to your continuin' good fortune . . . stayin' above ground,' he toasted.

They drank and Henner refilled the glasses. He took two cheroots from a top pocket, offered one to Cal, who refused.

'I'm wonderin' how much there is to you, Crow,' he pondered aloud.

'Nothin' more'n you know already,' Cal answered.

Henner blew out a match, watched the thin curl of smoke. He shrugged.

'A bindle stiff who's looking for a man . . . two men to kill. Methinks there's more to you than that, friend.' He considered the end of his cheroot. 'What were you before? What'll you be after?'

'Unless you're on the trail o' Border Troopers, I could ask the same o' you, Henner. But I ain't that interested.'

Henner gave a nonchalant smile.

'I was only killin' time, till the stage loads up . . . which is about now. It ain't goin' to be no clambake. It's a twelve hour run to Sego Bench.' Henner's eyes moved away from Cal to near the batwing doors. 'But right now we've somethin' else to think about,' he said.

Cal turned to see a big man had entered the saloon. Head and shoulders above most, his pale eyes moved over the crowd. He saw Henner and Cal, held their gaze as he walked forward. He was mature-tough and craggy, wore thick moustaches that covered the bottom half of his face. He was the man Cal had stood back for on the boardwalk, had a silver star pinned to his waist-coat.

'Evenin' Marshal,' Henner acknowledged, quickly.

The marshal's discerning eyes picked over Cal's face.

'There's a feller outside gettin' dust in his beard,' he stated. 'An' he's got a rip bigger'n Apache Pass in his gut.'

Then he spoke to Henner.

'I'm only guessin' at *your* business, citizen, but the stage leaves in fifteen minutes. Don't miss it.'

The marshal turned his attention back to Cal.

'We get three, maybe four shootin's on a busy night. Most o' that's what you might call domestic . . . family feuds . . . hot blood. I suggest you ride around Las Cruces next time.'

There was something about the marshal made Cal's skin crawl. He spoke softly. 'I ain't got no family, but I doubt I'll be passin' this way again, Marshal.'

The marshal remained impassive.

'The stage . . . be on it,' he returned flatly. 'I'll have a word with the driver. You won't need tickets.'

The marshal turned away and moved through the crowd, didn't look back.

'Wouldn't like to see *him* in bad humour,' Henner suggested.

Almost reluctantly, both men finished their whiskies and walked from the busy saloon. Henner paused, flicked the butt-end of his cheroot into the street.

You see the gun he was totin'?' he said. 'Looked like a Sharps carbine . . . short-tooled in a custom holster. It must o' reached to his knee. Like the man said: make sure you ride around next time.'

In front of the stage office the big, concord coach stood ready, its team fully harnessed, the running lights glowing. The straps of the luggage boot were down and the overweight driver was loading an assortment of bags. A man in a derby hat stomped irritably about him.

The driver's voice sounded unaccommodating and final.

'I'm as patient as the next man, Prof, but if you don't shut your belly-achin' I'll toss you an' your rotgut elixirs out for Marshal Lome to deal with.'

'Snake-oil peddler,' Henner said. 'Another outcast. We're in good company.'

There were two men already sitting in the stage. One was grinning at the argument in the street, the other sat unmoved, staring straight ahead. Cal thought he knew the face, a shadow from the past. Cold and unresponsive, the man looked towards him, then turned away.

Henner, saw Cal's fleeting interest.

'You know him?' he asked.

'Dunno . . . maybe.'

'Let's hope for his sake, you don't.'

Henner pulled himself up on to the step, swung inside the coach. He sat next to the man at the window. Cal followed, then the medicine drummer climbed in. His face was pinched, had the mien of someone who hadn't found much to his liking in Las Cruces.

The driver's heavy jowelled face appeared in the doorway.

'Get secure,' he advised. 'I'll be givin' the team some leather . . . non-stop to the Lordsburg relay.'

Then the marshal called out. 'Hold up, Chubby. You've got room for another. Our good ladies have been spring-cleaning.'

Cal poked his head from the coach. In the light from a lamp outside the stage office he saw a girl, caught a glimpse of chestnut-coloured hair and a pale face.

The marshal strode from the boardwalk to talk to her. He gestured anxiously, had a quick look back along the street.

'It's nothin' to do with me, Lauren,' he said. 'It's just there's some ladies have decided Las Cruces can do without you. Let me give you a hand.'

The girl looked hard at the marshal.

'That's very appropriate Denton,' she said, cryptically, and gave a sour smile.

Lauren Garth stepped into the coach, sat next to the so-called professor. She had a glance at her fellow passengers, then poked her hand out the side window. She stuck a finger in the air, mouthed something foul at Marshal Denton Lome and his town.

'You tell 'em, gal,' Henner said.

The girl dashed off a sneer that included Cal, then the marshal was back at the door.

'I meant what I said, Lauren. It weren't my decision,' he said.

Lauren pulled a shawl around her shoulders.

'Get yourself a wife,' she shouted into the street. 'Be a goddamn hypocrite for the rest of your natural.'

27

The marshal bristled when he heard suppressed sniggers from the men in the coach. He stepped up close to the open door.

'There's some fine company here,' he rasped. 'We got a frail sister, a quack salesman, a cow thief an' a butcher who ain't too fussy where he sticks his knife.'

The marshal spat blatantly into the ground, turned his back on the coach.

Cal leaned forward and goaded him. 'Yeah, maybe that's right, but none of us sounds like a mare's arse.'

Lome stopped and turned slowly.

Cal smiled, shook his head. 'If you didn't have that piece of artillery tied to your hock, an' state law to back you up, I'd be tempted to stick you with some manners, Lawman.'

Lome took a step back and took off his Stetson, held it against his massive chest.

'In that case, you just forget what I said about givin' the town a miss. Make sure you call in an' see me next time you're in this neck o' the woods. You hear me, stranger?' he threatened.

'My name's Crow. Calvin Crow,' Cal said calmly, as Lome turned and walked away.

When Cal spoke, the marshal hesitated. No one noticed, but for a brief moment his features froze before he continued.

The well-fed driver smiled at Lauren, winked at Cal.

'Midnight ... time to roll, you darlin' people,' he bellowed, as he slammed the door shut. Then he climbed up to his seat and the stagecoach swayed with his weight. He released the brake, called the moving-off ritual to his team.

The marshal was back on the boardwalk and his eyes bored searchingly into Cal.

'That's one you ain't left dead, Crow,' Henner pointed out drily. 'You might live to regret it. We all might. He ain't of a disposition to forget tonight. And he's a big, mean son of a bitch.'

Cal was returning Lome's oppressive authority.

'Yeah. I think you're right on all counts,' he muttered.

# 4
# Lordsburg

The stage rolled away from the shanties at the end of town and Lauren Garth moved restlessly in her seat. She was sitting opposite Cal, could just see that he was watching her.

Cal was wondering about her. He liked her style, her resilience and it moved him to smile.

Henner's snake-oil peddler was dabbing at his face with a handkerchief.

'I can't understand that marshal . . . that town. I've done nobody there any harm,' he said miserably.

'Other than those kickin' up greasewood,' Henner laughed.

The amiable man grinned, and let his eyes stray around the coach, shook his head.

'From what the marshal was sayin', I'd be worried about the company I was keepin', if it wasn't for the lady,' he said, still with a smile on his face.

'You can always get out an' walk, mister,' Cal said, quietly.

Henner screwed up his face, muttered an exasperated oath.

'This is goin' to be some trip,' Lauren said, catching the mood.

'Yeah, well we might as well get acquainted,' the smiling man said. 'I'm Jared Munroe,' He looked at the others.

'Doctor Chirp,' said the medicine drummer.

'I'm Lauren,' the girl offered. 'But then you already know that.'

She looked at Cal. 'I enjoyed your conversation with Denton Lome. Was that from the safety of the coach, or are you always that brave?'

Cal almost chuckled. 'The safety of the coach,' he answered, then he lapsed into silence. He was trying to place the man who still hadn't spoken.

Behind them, the lights of Las Cruces twinkled and faded into nothing. Heading west, they settled to an even pace; the rolling groan and squeak of the coach harmonizing with the drumming of the horses' hoofs.

In the darkness, Doctor Chirp coughed, licked his lips noisily. Those not already asleep heard the unmistakable peep of a cork being twisted, the gurgle of liquid.

'That bug-juice'll likely kill you before we get to Lordsburg,' Henner said, then added, 'but it don't look like death ever done you any harm. Give us a swig.'

'No,' Chirp retorted, and the coach went back to its intimate silence.

In the featureless scrape of the Sonoran desert the running lights made occasional flickers across the passengers' faces. The run was into the day's first hours, and a few words of the driver's song wafted down on the night breeze.

Oh, Susanna,
Now don't you cry for me.
I'm bound for Alabamy,
With my banjo on my knee.

'That's pretty . . . he sings good,' Lauren said.

'Yeah, he does. I think it's an old rebel song. You know it?' Cal asked.

'I've heard most songs in my business.'

'What exactly is that?' Cal asked, without an overtone.

'Amongst other things, I'm the "frail sister" the marshal mentioned. You forgot already?'

Cal's mouth opened, closed quickly – and Lauren smiled.

'You were thinkin' the marshal made a mistake. Maybe it was some other trouble got me pushed out of Las Cruces?'

'No, ma'am. I hadn't thought *anythin'* about you,' he lied.

Cal closed his eyes again. He thought he'd said enough – realized how long it had been since he'd talked to a woman.

After half an hour or so, Cal opened his eyes. He watched the indigo moon-shadow of the coach move across the alkali flatness. He thought back, troubled at being told to leave town. It hadn't happened to him before.

Disturbed thoughts filled Cal's mind, frustrated him into tiredness. He drifted into a fitful sleep, the onset of the voice already in his head. It was the unfailing return of his nightmare: 'I'm cold. Don't let me die, Pa' – Walker's plaintive cry to be saved.

Cal couldn't figure whether it had been minutes, hours or days even, but he came to at the snap of traces, when the brakes went on. The brighter glow of oil lamps flashed through the coach windows, and he blinked at the sleep-puffed features of those around him. The stage pulled to a halt, swayed on its axles as Chubby climbed down.

'Lordsburg,' he called out. 'We got one hour. There's food an' hot coffee.'

Cal opened the coach door and stiffly climbed down. He turned and held out his hand for Lauren. She hesitated a moment then smiled, allowed him to steady her to the ground.

Henner followed, then Chirp.

'At the price we paid for this trip, you'd think the company would invest in cushioned seats,' he complained.

Munroe climbed out, grinning as usual. He was the cow-thief, Cal decided. The man looked to the distant horizon. 'I smell some serious weather comin' in,' he said.

The man Denton Lome hadn't mentioned in his appraisal of the passengers was the last to come out. He looked at Cal, spoke for the first time.

'I don't like the way you keep lookin' at me.'

'I don't either. What I like less, is why I keep doin' it,' Cal told him.

Henner laughed, said quietly to Cal, 'You're a man with few sides, Crow.'

The Lordsburg relay station was a square, adobe-walled, sod-roofed building. It had outbuildings; one was a kitchen, the other was home for the Mexican family who tended it.

Inside the station, a bar was fashioned along one side, had a colourful mural painted on the wall behind it. The stagecoach passengers were seated around a long table away from the door. Cal had a look around him, saw the quiet man wasn't in the room. Henner sat beside Lauren Garth who glanced covertly at Cal.

Cal ate his meal of eggs, ham and fried potatoes in silence. When he'd finished, he took a biscuit and a mug of coffee outside. It was approaching dawn and streaks of pink and grey were reaching out from the east. Cal leaned against the adobe, watched the brightening sky.

'It's peaceful,' Lauren Garth said, walking up beside him. 'Do you mind if I stand here?'

'No, ma'am. Why do you ask?'

'Someone like me usually has to.'

Cal looked at her, interested. 'You feel bitter about Las Cruces?'

'No. I've been kicked out of horse-towns all the way from Dallas. East of there, they've become respectable. But I've had my times. Perhaps Sego Bench will be more broad-minded.' Lauren gave Cal a wistful look. 'Do you think *you'll* find what you're lookin' for in Sego?' she asked.

Cal looked into the last of his coffee. 'If Marshal Lome moves on all whom he judges trash . . . yes, ma'am, reckon I will,' he said.

He touched his Stetson, walked away quietly. He stood in the early light and watched the relay man adjusting the harness of the new team.

Within five minutes, Chubby Pound came out of the station.

'All aboard who's comin' aboard,' he called.

The passengers walked out to the coach. Chirp was first aboard followed by Lauren, whom Munroe stepped aside for. Then Henner came out and Chubby yelled to move off.

'Lets go, people.'

Cal didn't move. He was uneasy, suspicious because the quiet man hadn't appeared. He was still inside the station.

With his left hand, Cal unbuttoned his coat. Then with his right, he fingered the corded hilt of the beaver-knife. The coach was ready and the team were eager, restless as they walked away from the building. Chubby called out again.

'You two fellers goin' to get aboard? You ain't goin' anywhere on foot from here.'

Suddenly, from the station doorway, which was just behind and to the side of Cal, the quiet man spoke.

'I've been jawin' with your friend. He tells me you kill Border Troopers, Crow. Kill 'em for fun.'

Cal turned slowly to face the man.

'He's wrong. I take it real serious. You got a name?' he asked.

'Yeah. "Boss".'

Then Cal remembered. All the time, it had been in the dark recesses of his mind. The man was from Barkdale. He'd been a guard, but Cal didn't recall, couldn't make anything other than that, and he told the man.

'I guess it ain't you I want. But if I ever remember otherwise . . .'

For a brief moment, Cal let the implied threat hang in the air, then he added; 'Unless you can't take the worry, then we'd best settle it now.'

'And how the hell you figure on doin' that, *snuffy?*' the man said threateningly.

Cal was going to show him when the man fired. It was a sharp detonation, a bright flash of flame. But Cal had estimated the move and already twisted away.

The man knew his gun was only effective at short range, and that's how it was for Cal and his massive-bladed knife. His mind raced as the blast caught him. But the bullet missed and he knew his next move had to be quick. He didn't want to make a fuss, and the coach was more than impatient to leave.

In one movement he pulled the knife and powered his arm down, felt the terrible thump as the blade struck. He cursed silently as the man gasped, swore again and lashed out with his foot. He caught the crumpling man in the chest, thrust him into the ground. He saw the gush of dark blood at the half-severed wrist, the hand still clasped around a short-barrelled Colt. He looked down at the man's contorted face, shuddered at the mouth that opened and closed in hushed agony.

He thrust his knife into its sheath, then kneeled in the dust.

'We ever meet again, I'll saw your head off . . . slowly,' he hissed.

Across the station yard, Chubby had twisted around in his seat. He looked back at the sound of the scuffle.

'What's the shootin' about? Where's the other feller?' he called down as Cal came briskly towards him.

'He ain't comin' . . . suddenly don't feel too good. We should get goin'.'

Cal climbed aboard the already moving coach.

'He won't be feelin' much at all,' he muttered under

his breath. He sat in the Border Trooper's seat, looked tiredly at Franklin Henner. 'You sure got a big mouth, Henner. Just don't ever tell me, *you* were one o' them Troopers.'

Henner made appeasing noises, fidgeted with a copy of the stagecoach company's news-sheet.

The stage swung out again into the desert, picked up speed. Cal went within himself, closed his eyes. A nerve in his right arm began to tremble and after a while he fell into a shallow sleep.

Lauren Garth's head was dropped, and her breathing was soft and regular. But from under her lowered eyelids, she was watching the sleeping man's face and Henner knew it.

'Maybe I *should* have kept my mouth shut,' he said quietly. 'He's livin' to avenge the death of his boy. I guess somehow I wanted to help him. That blue-ticket scum didn't have a chance. No one from Barkdale does.'

Lauren wondered how different Henner was from the man who sat opposite her. Henner had *some* feeling – an attribute she hadn't seen in Crow. But then it seemed *he* had a reason.

'Is there anyone for you in Sego ... friends ... family?' she asked.

'No. No one. You?'

'If there are, they won't be friends or family.'

'Why don't we start somethin' together ... break open a new deck? We could open up a gamblin' room ... a gamblin' *tent* perhaps? Henner winked at his conjecture.

Lauren's eyes brightened in the thin early light. 'Hmmm,' she said, 'I'm interested. Of course, it'll have to be a fifty-fifty partnership, and I'm only workin' from an honest house.'

Henner nodded, curiously earnest. 'Yes ma'am,' he agreed. 'We'd work on a house percentage. That's good enough. We'd just have to make it last.'

'You got me real excited, Mr Henner.' But Lauren didn't feel greatly confident of a partnership with Franklin Henner; not much enthusiasm for a new beginning. And that had something to do with Calvin Crow.

# 5

# Workings of Sego Bench

The stage lurched through a furrowed draw, and Cal opened his eyes. Brilliant light filled the coach, and he squinted at the immense prairie of paintbrush and white sego.

Chirp muttered something about 'This God-forsaken place'.

Cal rubbed his aching neck-muscles. The other passengers were stirring, restless to get somewhere. Henner yawned noisily and rubbed his eyes.

'I wonder what excitement this fine-looking day will bring,' he said.

Cal looked at Lauren. He didn't think she'd slept much, probably too much on her mind. He gave a furtive smile, and she reciprocated.

Munroe swung a leg out straight, banged it vigorously with his fist.

'Hey, Genuine Jimmy,' he said mischievously to Chirp. 'How come arms and legs find time to sleep, when a head don't?'

The heat inside the coach was cruel and building up. It was close to midday, when Chubby shouted.

'Sego Bench . . . twenty minutes.'

Cal leaned from the window, looked ahead. They were nearing the deep-notched foothills of the Nama Altos Mountains.

From a distance, the outskirts of Sego Bench looked like a spread of prairie dog mounds; mud houses among prickly pear and broom that hid the town proper.

After ten minutes the coach was through the rude dwellings, into the tents and pole cabins of the roaring camp that hugged the wagon road east of town.

On the flat stretch of land that gave the town half its name, framed buildings edged the main street. Men with slouch hats and long beards talked excitedly in groups, and a steady traffic of freight-wagons and tool carts plied the street.

North of the town, the walls of a steep-sided arroyo were dotted with mine tailings, where shafts had been driven into the loose rock of silver workings. Below and parallel to that, curled the waters of San Simon Creek.

The stage pulled up outside a false-fronted building that backed the arroyo wall. Jared Munroe spat vigorously to the ground.

'I can smell prospect,' he growled.

'When we pulled into Lordsburg, he said he could smell "serious weather",' Henner murmured. 'Let's hope he's right this time. All *I* can smell is crap.'

Cal got up, grimaced at his stiffness. He swung open the door beside him and climbed down. He lifted his hand for Lauren. She raised her head and looked around at the hectic, squalid business of Sego Bench, made a poor show of hiding her dismay.

The driver clambered down from his seat. He was humming, then whistling, then grinning.

'Money. They're diggin' it out o' the ground,' he said excitedly.

Henner climbed out quietly. He studied the sprawl of the town, then looked at Lauren. 'Rich pickings for everyone ... includin' us.' His voice sounding more encouraged.

Munroe stepped down quickly behind Lester Chirp. 'I got a deal ... someone to see,' he said doubtfully, and without any further word or explanation walked off.

The driver unstrapped the luggage boot and rolled up the canvas cover. He handed down a large leather valise to Chirp who was already thinking of moving on.

'Mariposa Hotel, across the street. Rooms an' the biggest an' best food in town,' he advised.

As he spoke, a man appeared in the doorway of the hotel. The man, who was hatless and sweaty, stepped forward on to the boardwalk, then down to the wheel-rutted street.

'Chubby Pound,' he called out, raised his hand cheerily. 'On time to join the partying. The north face deposits showed last week. There's been some rich finds here, Chubby.'

Chubby chuckled. 'On time, it would seem, Lyle. I've just made my last run. The company's sendin' a driver. He'll pick up the coach from Jimes's Livery ... take it right back to El Paso. Yessir, I've waited many moons to hear that news, my friend.'

41

Lyle smiled broadly. 'You folks get yourselves off the street,' he told the passengers. 'Food's always ready. Breakfast, dinner or supper, it's a dollar a plate. There's no beds left though, not here. The town's full to bustin'.'

Cal felt the press of concern amongst the others, but his personal vow to seek out Krewel and Gibson still burned inside him. From what he'd heard, Sego Bench was a likely place to find them, so for the moment, food and bedding mattered little. Like Munroe, he had nothing to explain, and he turned his back on them.

Lauren watched him as he began his walk along the street, then Franklin Henner took her arm. She looked at him, surprised, then her smile turned casual.

'You don't waste any time,' she said. 'But I guess someone better start dealing.'

Cal paced himself slowly in the main street's sweltering heat. The sun was muscling down, burning up the town's detritus and Henner was right; the smell was overpowering. There was only patchy shade; along the boardwalk some of the buildings had pieces of tent canvas stretched into makeshift awnings.

The town was filled with the buzz of improvement and growth. Lumber-wagons rolled in from distant timberlines. They were laden with green pine for the founding of new stores and mining shanties.

Cal avoided the townsfolk; mostly miners, whose theme of conversation was the potential of their claim, the objects of their fortunes.

Most of the buildings along the main street were single storey and clap-boarded. From the front, pent roofs of bleached canvas stretched to the rear.

The Stack Saloon was a crude, loose-planked structure. It stood alone at the far end of the main street, looked as though a big desert wind could blow it straight to California.

Floor-to-ceiling shutters had been drawn to one side, and Cal crossed the threshold. The reek of sour beer and stale sweat enveloped him and he blinked, shook himself. The one big room was shoaling with workmen, but he pushed through to where two bartenders were filling beer-glasses.

In each corner of the room, there was a table with men gambling. At one end, there was a long table set near to the wall with three men seated behind it, They were working the horns and assay-scales, paying out to the miners who were having their pokes valued.

At the bar, where a grain of silver ore was worth one bit, Cal put a dollar down and got a glass of beer. There was no change and he wasn't of a mind to question the inflated price. He picked up his warm drink and moved cautiously, drifted naturally with the crowd. Within ten minutes he found himself back beside the tall front shutters. He loitered for a few more moments while he drained his glass.

Cal was sure Krewel and Gibson weren't in the saloon and, as in Las Cruces, he decided to visit a few more drinking-holes along the street. It was approaching first dark when he emerged from Bernie's Bar, having nearly worked his way back to where he'd alighted from the stage.

He stood quietly watching the town. Torches were already burning outside some buildings and Cal thought the through traffic was getting heavier, more eager in its movement. He looked to the north, saw tiny pinpricks of light across the darkening arroyo slope. For a brief moment, all the twinkling lights of the miners' claims shaded his single-mindedness.

The remembering stayed longer. It was the reek of decaying rubbish swirling low through the town's underpinning that reminded him of the stench of Barkdale. He bunched his fists as the sweating started, as the memories trampled across his mind.

It was Crick Gibson who'd callously tossed a blanket over Walker, hours, maybe minutes before he'd died; Jeeter Krewel who'd put the livid scar on Cal's forehead with the barrel of a big Colt. Barkdale had meant nothing to those men, other than a means to make a dollar. Robbing, then burying men and boys, whose only crime had been to get within rounding-up distance.

Cal stared at the dirty bearded faces that passed him by. He wondered if he'd really know Krewel and Gibson if he saw them again. But he'd known Dillard Groff that night on the bridge outside of Langtry; the guard who'd beaten Walker to death with a cow-pole. Yeah, he'd remembered *him* all right. Perhaps Cal had killed him too quickly, with too little pain.

Cal sniffed wood-smoke, heard some coarse laughter nearby. A banjo plucked out a tinny tune, and outside the Mariposa Hotel a pariah dog was fighting for the right to a beef-bone.

'I'll remember 'em. I got nothin' else to do,' he muttered, and the thought bleakly reassured him.

From somewhere up among the mine-workings he heard the faint knocking of props being hammered into rock. He was considering his next move when Jared

Munroe almost bumped into him. Munroe started, obviously recognized Cal, but stepped past him, down into the street.

Cal shrugged. The thrown-together alliance, the brief sojourn between towns was over. None of the passengers from Las Cruces was anything more than an outcast. For various reasons, they'd all unceremoniously dumped themselves at Sego Bench. He thought of Lauren Garth, went over the words he'd exchanged with her. Suddenly he felt very isolated, realized it was his interest in her, the price he paid because he wasn't going to do anything about it.

He had a few seconds of extreme swearing, then went back into the bar.

# 6
# Table Stakes

In the Mariposa Hotel, Franklin Henner finished the last of his rib-eye steaks and dabbed at his lips, looked across the table. Lauren Garth's eyes were sleepy, half closed. He watched her hands, unmoving.

'I thought it was makin' money that interested you, Mr Henner . . . Franklin?' she said, her face lifting, suddenly more wakeful.

'Frank,' Henner corrected, smiling. 'Yes, it is. I was just wonderin' how difficult . . . or easy it would be for us.' He took a cheroot from his pocket, bit off the end and lit it.

'To do what?'

'To buy a plot. We'll have to put up a frame, get a tarp stretched. That's goin' to take more'n a few days.'

Lauren tut-tutted, shook her head. Her eyes looked very dark in her pale face.

'I said, I'd work in an honest *house*, not an honest *tent*,' she said. 'Anyways I don't have time for that. My flush has been busted. There's buildings almost ready-made at the end of town.'

Henner nodded. 'Yeah, so are the men who own 'em.'

Lauren laughed. 'You've got money, Frank. You're goin' to have to put some of it up front. How much you got?'

Henner blew smoke, looked at her through it.

'A little over a thousand,' he answered. 'Look, Miss Lauren—' he went on.

'Are you serious about this or not?' she broke in. 'Make up your mind, Frank. And my name's Lauren. Forget the "Miss". What's the best lookin' house in town?' she asked.

'For what you . . . we want . . . I'd say the place called Black Jack's,' he said. 'It's a big spread an' it must've cost big money. I'll go an' see someone. You stay here. I'll get us set up . . . get you a room, even.'

Lyle Roach was sweating a little more than usual. His face was shining in the light from a glass-shaded lamp where he sat at his desk in the hotel's foyer. He didn't look up as Henner approached him. He was engrossed in a tattered copy of an aged Tucson newspaper.

Henner laughed. 'Them Texicans still holdin' out at The Alamo?' he asked in a friendly manner.

Roach looked up and sniggered. 'Don't say,' he answered. 'Reckon they're savin' that kinda news for next year.'

Henner smiled, pulled out a silver dollar.

'Nine more o' these, says you've got a room for a woman who's riding lonesome. Seems this town's crowded her out.'

Roach squinted considerably at the coin. 'That's true. I'd have to give her my own room.'

Henner laid the coin down. 'Whatever. As long as you ain't in it,' he said.

Roach sniffed, thought about the offer. 'I could get ten times that,' he said.

'No you couldn't. I know who needs a bed, an' they ain't got pennies to rub. I'll give you twenty.'

Henner pulled two notes from an inside pocket, laid them down in front of Roach.

'My room's built out back,' the hotel keeper said. 'It don't look much from the outside, but inside . . . well. It's secure enough too.'

Henner smiled. 'Yeah, like the US Treasury,' he said, mockingly. 'You go tell Miss Garth she's got a room for the night. I'll be back later.'

Henner crossed the foyer and left the hotel. He stood on the edge of the boardwalk, flicked away the remains of his cheroot. The chill breeze made him shiver, but things were happening and his face broke into a lean grin.

Black Jacks stood in its own plot, further down the street. It featured the ubiquitous, gaudy false front and rose a floor higher than any other building on the bench. Along the front, big flaming lamps burned off the night, and a tout shouted for trade.

Henner watched the routine, studied the street and the mêlée coming in and out of the building. Under the boardwalk, almost beneath his feet, two drunks lay in the dust. They were curled up close, and they shivered. One of them whimpered as he slept.

The gambler flexed his shoulders and went through the batwing doors; into the pungency that smothered him like an old pillow.

At one end of the enormous room, standing on an upturned cart, a girl in a lace-trimmed corset revealed her sturdy white legs while she sang 'Turkey in the Straw'. Bawdy catcalls and slapped applause encouraged her performance, and she smirked her way into another chorus.

Interested, Henner watched for a moment, then he pushed his way to the long-running bar. It was a heavy construction and ran for forty feet across the rear of the building, was three men deep from end to end. Four bartenders were providing a rapid service, but it wasn't keeping up. A drunken brawl erupted and some glasses were smashed. But it went unnoticed by practically everyone except the house wranglers who moved in purposefully. There were two of them and Henner approved of the way they dispatched the rabble-rousers head first through a side door.

He ordered himself a glass of beer and sipped it slowly, looking around him. There was a bead curtain at the back of the room, at the end of the bar, that occasionally the bartenders went through. He gulped the last of the beer and, keeping close to the bar, pushed his way towards it. One of the bartenders noticed him, raised his chin enquiringly. Henner guessed the housemen had also seen him.

'Jack,' he said, with a touch of assurance. 'It's business.'

The man nodded and Henner coughed, disguised his relief. He brushed the curtain aside, saw the glass-panelled doors ahead of him. He knocked once at the one with a light burning, opened the door and stepped inside.

A man seated at a big desk looked up as Henner pushed the door to, behind him. He was a big man, and although distracted, the features of his black face remained inscrutable.

'What do you want?' he said flatly.

Amusement showed in Henner's face.

'Yeah, Black Jack's,' he said, 'I shoulda guessed. Some action's what I want, Jack.'

Jack looked slightly baffled, closed the book that lay open on the desk. He shoved his chair back and stood up, ready to put an immediate end to any trouble.

'You seen the tables outside? Something wrong with them?' This time there was a warning in his voice.

Henner shook his head, smiled agreeably.

'No. Not if you're after weaner sport.'

'I know you came in on the Las Cruces stage,' Jack responded coolly. 'You get moved on by that tough marshal?'

Henner took a step further into the room.

'Not me personally. But I didn't want to push my luck.'

Jack thought for a second. 'Yeah, you never wanna do that, friend,' he said. 'Perhaps I can oblige. Come back at ten o'clock. Bring a name and a stake.'

'I'll do that,' Henner answered. Satisfied, he went back to the saloon bar.

Watching play at the black-jack and faro tables, he waited for close on an hour. Like Lauren Garth, he could assess a good house-percentage. Standing at the bar, he figured the 'take' in his head and smiled hungrily. Then, within a space of ten minutes he saw three men go through the curtain, but he waited until the time Jack had told him.

In the room adjoining the office, the players were already seated around Jack's private poker-table when Henner entered. He nodded.

'Good evening. My name's Henner. Frank Henner,' he introduced himself.

With a striking display of ornate silver, Jack's hand indicated the others at the table.

'Mel Priddle. Ronson Bale. Clooney Piper.'

Henner removed his hat. 'Gentlemen,' he said, and took the fifth chair.

'We play table stakes,' Jack said, and poured whiskey. He carried the glasses to the table. 'Dealer's choice. There's sealed packs an' the liquor's on me.'

Mel Priddle finished building himself a cigarette. 'Gimme some cards,' he responded. He looked a dour man; a man of the open range, not a miner.

Jack grunted, laid a deck of cards on the table and took his chair.

Ronson Bale sat on Henner's right. He was heavy set with a tangle of mutton-chops and his hands were thick and muscled. Henner thought he looked like the business end of freighting.

Clooney Piper was the easier mark. He was wary and probably a capper for the house – Jack's house. Henner smiled contentedly and filed some reference. Put the squeeze on Piper, he reckoned, and the man would hem and haw without Jack's backing.

The first hand came down and Henner studied the players, went with the play and made no effort to win. As he thought, Piper played it tight, bowed out when he was pushed. Priddle was impulsive, liked to take a plunge. Ronson Bale was harder to judge, had no marked pattern of play. He came in on a whim, and that worried Henner.

Jack was the calm professional, a gambler who made his own cut-off point. He liked the cards to do their own work, made light use of the bluff. But he had a fault: he enjoyed the raising too much on a pat hand. To Henner that was a good sign. It meant the man wouldn't enjoy going up against a bad one. He was satisfied he'd know when Jack was bluffing.

Henner shrewdly measured his play. After an hour of losing, he took until midnight to get even. Then for another hour he started to build his winnings. Mel Priddle was on the way out. He'd lost steadily, and drank heavily. As his voice became more slurred, so his playing became erratic, and he bluffed openly. Henner hoped he'd keep going.

It was one o' clock in the morning, and the small room was thick with tobacco smoke. Jack kept the glasses filled, although Henner had only drained his twice. He estimated he was ahead a few thousand dollars, knew trouble was on the way when Jack and Piper traded nervous glances.

Beads of sweat glistened on Jack's tense face and for the first time he took a big slug of his whiskey.

Piper stretched his arms, scraped his chair back from the table.

'I'm stiffer'n a witch's finger,' he said. 'Goin' to stretch my legs.'

'You ain't goin' anywhere, goddamnit. Sit down,' Henner rasped.

The capper looked at Henner, then at Jack, who shrugged, before he slumped back down.

'You're a mite spooky,' Piper said.

'I'm a mite careful,' Henner told him.

Ronson Bale grinned at Piper. 'You pick your times, Clooney,' he said and chortled.

'We came here to play cards. Let's get on with it,' Priddle garbled.

Bale swallowed his whiskey. 'Yeah, let's,' he said. 'An' if I wanted ten-dollar pots, Jack I'd have stayed out front. It's time we upped the stakes.'

Jack nodded and reached for a new deck. Henner saw a furtive look pass between the saloon-owner and Piper. He guessed they were going to make a move on him, but he was ahead and would get in first.

Jack expertly shuffled the cards with a new-found assurance.

'When cards begin, friendship ends,' he said smiling, pushing the deck across the table for Henner to cut.

Henner returned the smile, and reached for the cards. His ran his fingertips along the sides of the pack, felt the shaving. Without hesitating or losing his smile, he cut the deck in the middle. But he also coughed, strident and stagey. He swore and apologized, drew the half-pack he'd lifted, towards him. With his other hand, he dragged a big kerchief from his top pocket. With a flourish he cleared his throat, wiped his mouth and replaced the kerchief.

'Sorry gentlemen,' he said. 'It's these night breezes. Who knows what they're bringin' in from that goddamn pole camp east o' town.'

The other men looked at each other uneasily, but didn't say anything. Henner placed the cards back near the centre of the table, saw Jack looking at him with a perceptive look in his eyes.

Yeah, that's right, I switched half the deck. Now you can start sweatin' again, Henner thought, almost said aloud.

Jack ground his teeth, slowly picked up the deck. The cards Henner had switched were twenty, maybe thirty cards deep. That meant that in dealin' from the bottom, Jack wouldn't know what cards he was drawing. Jack thoughtfully placed the first cards around the table.

Ronson Bale opened the pot for a hundred dollars, Piper followed and Henner came in blind. When all cards were down he picked up his hand, fanned it slow. Four hearts; the deuce, trey, four and the five. He closed the cards and thought about the chances of the ace or six turning up.

Mel Priddle was miserable because he couldn't even tag along. He'd lost most of his stake, was down to less than the required hundred dollars. The betting was suddenly too strong for him and he made his excuses, bowed out of the game.

Jack had his eye on Henner, considered his choices: get beaten by luck, or wait. Henner watched him making up his mind, then Jack pushed his bet forward.

Bale and Piper took two cards each and Henner indicated one, saw the ebb and flow of Jack's expression. The dealer placed a card in front of Henner and frowned when it wasn't picked up, took a single card for himself.

Within moments, Bale was leading again.

'Two hundred,' he said, with a wry smile.

Piper sneered, but followed on.

Without looking at his draw card, Henner counted out the money, led Jack in with the call.

Jack hesitated once again, then he equalled the bet.

54

'There's your two hundred, and eight more,' he said.

Bale glanced at Henner, then at Jack.

'That's eleven hundred you're in for,' he said. 'That's real brave, Jack.'

'And aggressive,' Henner muttered.

Bale shrugged, decided to stay in the game.

Henner was looking confidently at the cards in his hand.

'I'm goin' to stay with these. They look real pretty,' he said with a challenging smile. 'So pretty, I'm goin' to back 'em with a thousand more.'

'That's me finished.' Piper closed his eyes and pushed his chair unsteadily away from the table, dragged on his cigarette.

Jack chewed his bottom lip, jingled the big gold rings on his left hand against his whiskey glass.

'That's a bet from someone who's ahead on the table, an' I ain't fallin' for it,' he said determinedly. 'If you want to play against me, it'll cost you another three thousand.'

Henner kept the flicker of satisfaction from his face. He's fallen for it, he thought.

Bale looked from Jack to Henner and closed his hand, tossed the cards down in front of them.

'Too rich for me, goddamnit,' he said with a sigh.

Jack glared at Henner. 'You said you wanted action, well now you're gettin' it,' he said harshly.

'I did, an' I meant it,' Henner told him, his face deadpan. 'Now, if you want to play against *me*, it'll cost you another *five* thousand.'

Jack chuckled. 'I ain't got that much cash in front o' me, an' you know it,' he said, a little less confident.

Henner gave a very thin smile. He knew that Jack had reached his cut-off point, the limit of the real value of his cards. Now Henner would have to make the killing, help it along with an irritation chaser.

'You've protected yourself with table-stakes, tinhorn. But I'm the one with the cash in front o' me. Unless you want to fold in your own house, put up.' Henner looked around the smoky room. 'Write me a note on Black Jack's,' he added plainly.

There was no way Jack could have turned white, but Henner guessed he would if he could. Ronson Bale spluttered and shook himself awake, and Piper cursed, dropped the front legs of his chair to the ground.

They watched Jack's face, his big heavy features that broke into a concerned sweat. Then they saw the professional at work, reckoning the odds. Jack tugged at the collar of his shirt, had another look at the cards he held.

'I like your game, Frank,' he said. 'But I'm the one who bites pig.'

Jack reached for a discarded pack and ripped it apart. Bale handed him the stub of a pencil, and he wrote something on the square of torn paper. Bale had a quick look and signed it, gave it to Piper. The capper also wrote his name on it then shoved it into the pot.

'This is a big heap to lose Jack. I'd say it's just about everythin',' he suggested to the saloon-owner.

'Yeah, would be, if I was bluffin', or gamblin' even. But you boys know I never do that.' Jack stared coldly into Henner's face. 'Here's my four girls to prove it,' he said, laying down all the queens with an unwanted, unnecessary nine.

Henner sucked in air, winked cruelly at the man who

sat opposite him. His right hand dropped below the table as his left covered his cards. One at a time he turned them over; the two, three, four and five of hearts.

He touched the fifth card which he'd played blind throughout, returned Jack's cold stare.

'You're a chancer,' Jack hissed, the triumph written across his face.

'I reckon he's got the six,' Bale whispered.

'No. *I* was holdin' that. It's got to be the ace,' Piper said.

Henner turned over the ace of hearts.

'As I said, "real pretty",' he hissed back at Jack.

The muscles in the gambler's face twitched, his chest heaved and he got to his feet. He kicked out at his chair, sent it crashing across the room. His face contorted with anger, but Henner saw his mind working, saw him thinking back.

'You legged the deck, you son-of-a-bitch.' Jack took a step back and reached inside his grey frock-coat, pulled a belly gun.

Bale shuffled away from lines of fire, and Piper issued some panicky curses as Jack raised the gun.

Still seated, Henner sighed heavily as he brought up his left hand. He flexed a derringer into his palm and pulled the dual triggers simultaneously.

The explosion from the derringer reverberated wildly in the small room, cordite wisped into the pall of Piper's tobacco smoke.

'You knew . . . didn't bluff,' Jack breathed softly. 'You cheated me.' His bejewelled hand dropped the belly gun and he blinked slowly, tried to focus. Then he rocked forward, his blood seeping from the front of his fancy shirt. He fell across the table and his face stared lifeless, crushed the dollars of Henner's winnings.

Henner stared at him for a few seconds then got to his feet. He looked down with little sentiment.

'You were goin' to do it to me. But I wouldn't have shot you,' he said. He put the derringer in his pocket. 'This was for self-protection.'

Bale and Piper were watching him.

'If them miners an' their law an' order agency want to make somethin' o' this, you two are witnesses. Get someone in to sort this out . . . the game's closed,' he told them.

'I'll be makin' a few changes to the chorus line,' he quipped as he walked to the door. 'An' if you want to work the tables here, Piper, there'll be no more shaved decks. I've no room for any goddamn saddle-blanket gamblers.'

I promised Miss Lauren that, he thought to himself.

# 7
# Sleeping Partner

Lauren Garth sat on the low sofa in the foyer of the hotel. Her eyes flitted from the dust-grimed windows to the reception desk and threadbare floor covering. Lyle Roach appeared from a room behind his desk. He grinned and gave her a distressed newspaper.

'It ain't exactly news,' he said, 'but you can wipe your feet on it before gettin' into bed. The room ain't exactly Eastern style, but it's ready when you are.'

She thanked him, and remained seated for a while. Her mind was unsettled and she couldn't concentrate on anything she read below the old headlines. She heard the unmistakable sound of shooting, the yell of disorder from way up the street. She frowned at the noise, gave a stifled groan. Another town where the first gun to fire amounted to the law.

Would there ever be an end to those towns, Lauren wondered. She got up from the scuffed sofa just as a tall, dark, thin man angled towards her.

'Lauren. By cripes it *is* you,' he said. 'Does a man's eyes good. You're sure lookin' lovely. Real enjoyable.'

Lauren smiled up into the man's delighted face.

'You too, Pug,' she said. 'This hell-hole must agree with you.'

'Yep doody ma'am, it sure does. We agree with each other. I look like a bear, smell like a buffler most o' the time, though. But when you're workin' the claim I got, it's all sweet.'

'You here on your own, Pug?' she asked quietly.

'Yes ma'am,' the miner replied.

'So your wife an' kids'll be missin' you?'

'I guess so. I ain't written her in a dog's age.' Pug Edgcumbe perched a ham on the end of the sofa. 'Where you goin' to be, Lauren? You can put me down for a jig.'

She smiled indulgently. 'I'll be right here, Pug. But there's no more jiggin'.'

Pug looked surprised and his raw, tanned features suddenly reddened through his whiskers.

'Well, pardon me,' he said. 'You sure know how to hurt a man, Lauren. Yep, I'm gutted but pleased, if you understand?'

'Yeah. I think I know what you mean, Pug. I just hope it works out . . . that the road don't turn.'

Pug laughed gently. 'The road might. You just keep yourself straight, Miss Lauren. And if there's any way I can help. . . .'

As was often the case, Lauren was a little ahead of the miner.

'Why, yes there is, as it happens, Pug,' she said, pleasantly. 'Can you find me somewhere to peg? You obviously know the way things pan out.' She raised an eyebrow at her little pun.

For a moment, Pug thought on what she'd said.

'A claim? Your turnings ain't made for swingin' a pick, Lauren.'

'It's not for me. It's a friend I was thinkin' about.'

'I see. He's here ... along the bench, is he ... this friend?'

'Yeah, that's right, Pug. His name's Crow. Calvin Crow. If you could work something out, I'd be ... well you know,' she said almost shyly.

At that, Lauren said goodnight, and went thoughtfully to the room Lyle Roach had made available for her.

The room was small and musty, the ceiling tobacco-stained and low over the iron-framed bed. Some sheets and a blanket had been laid on a chair and she mindlessly pulled at them. There was an oil-lamp turned low, its weak light flickering Lauren's shadow across the clapboard walls. There was a slice of carved, black wood nailed up over the bed. It read:


'A man's dreams are his own.'


'Just as well,' Lauren muttered. She started to undress, saw herself in the framed mirror that stood on a wooden chest. Her hair looked good in the yellow light, but her pale face didn't: it showed the draw of sadness. She tried to blink away the picture, thought of Calvin Crow helping her down from the stagecoach. She covered herself in the sweat-stained sheets, for a long time lay restless and shivering. The night sounds of the town seeped through the thin walls and loneliness enveloped her.

It was well past midnight when she heard the light tapping at the door. She got up from the bed quickly, turned up the lamp which she'd deliberately kept low.

'Who is it?' she said, but she'd guessed.

'It's me, Frank. Let me in,' Henner said.

Lauren dragged the bolt from the door-frame. She took a step back and reached for the oil-lamp, let Henner open the door.

Warily, he stood in the doorway, just a bit drunk.

'You still got . . .' he started to say and stopped, changed his mind. 'I'm not comin' in. I just wanted to tell you we're in business. I took him, Lauren . . . nearly eight thousand. I got the house too. I'll show you . . . tomorrow.'

Lauren shook her head. 'You got the house?' she echoed, trying not to understand.

Henner swayed forward, made an impulsive grab for the bewildered girl. He grabbed her by an arm, but saw the oil-lamp, saw what she intended to do with it. He released her, backed off through the door.

'Sorry Lauren,' he said. 'But ol' Black Jack, he pulled a belly-gun on me. His death ain't goin' to sit too heavy . . . was self defence. I just did . . .' His voice croaked short as he pulled the door closed. His feet sounded steady as he went away, as though he'd rapidly got sober.

Lauren stood very still and shook. She could feel the hurt of his fingers on her arms, the sting of whiskeyed breath. She threw the door bolt, left the lamp up high and fell back on the bed. She'd been in town not much more than twelve hours and already the partner she'd cut from the pack had shot a man dead.

## The Black Road

Lauren pulled the blanket over her head, curled up in her cave of depression. Not for the first time she waited for the tears.

# 8
# Tough Decision

Early sunlight seeped through the clinkered walls of Jimes's Livery Stable. It touched Calvin Crow's face and stirred him to wakefulness. The night before, he'd stayed in Bernie's Bar till late, and for a moment he was beset with a vague sense of uncertainty. Then memory worked its curious charm and he laid back, closed his eyes for more time. Since its 'findings', Sego Bench was never fully asleep any more, and during the early hours made a steady clamour in Cal's head. He wondered what the day would bring, harked back to his boy, Walker. Eventually the thought of Krewel and Gibson tightened him, and he got to his feet.

He wanted to have a look at the north-face deposits. A good, close look by daylight. Southern Arizona was a vast land, with maybe a thousand silver, gold and copper mine workings. Any one of them could divert the two men he was seeking.

Hunger started to chew at his insides and he grimaced, brushed at the straw that clung to his crumpled clothes. He stepped carefully to the front of the stable, over men who were still sprawled asleep. It had cost Cal a dollar for a place to lie down, and it was, as the sharp hostler had informed him, a priceless blessing at that.

The first thing that Cal noticed when he stepped into the street was the smoky miasma that hung low along the bench of land above the town's buildings. It was approaching midday, and the street was crawling with an assortment of hauliers; push-and-pull drivers, sweating and cursing through another gruelling day.

From what Cal had overheard the night before, the silver finds were no flash in the pan. The north-face deposits could rival the Grant County copper-mines of sixty years ago. Within weeks, Sego Bench could double in size, in three months its numbers could rival the state capitol.

He stood watching the treasure hunters for a few minutes before he made a move. Just beyond the end of the street, another eat-and-get-out trough had opened. A painted board proclaimed:

TODAY THE FINEST FARE IN THE
TERRITORY $1. TOMORROW $2.

The canvas-topped structure had no front, and Cal waited in line to sit at one of the benches that faced a trestle-table. When his turn came, a gangly youth served him sourdough biscuits and gravy with sweet black coffee; all cold. He ate slowly, savouring the event, drank his coffee, and returned to the street.

He briefly had a look at every man's face as he passed them by, and the same doubt plagued him; would he know Krewel and Gibson if he found them?

It took him less than ten minutes to reach the Stack Saloon. Where the street ended at that end of town, a trader had erected a plank sign with the words:

DIG THE ENCHANTED GARDEN WITH
AN O'HAGAN SHOVEL.

It was an example of the legend that was sweeping thousands of miners away from the lure of the Rockies. The vision that led enterprising grubstakers to invest thousands of dollars. They laid fake veins with silver ore, then trumpeted riches for the gullible and greedy.

Cal was lost in thought, picking his way along the street, when he heard someone shout. He half-turned, then was slammed into the boardwalk, down on to his knees in the street dirt. He swore, reached for a hitching rail and pulled himself up, shook his head.

Above him two mounted men stared down. The rider who had swung his horse's hip into Cal grinned through an untidy beard.

'Mail-order cowboy,' he sneered.

The other man was small and had a hairless face, wore spectacles; both notable features in Sego Bench. As the two men pulled their horses away, he turned to confront Cal's embarrassment, gave a high-pitched snigger that Cal found curiously unnerving.

Cal remained calm. He dusted himself off again, looked irritated at his once smart garb. He spat into the dust.

'Just 'cause I ain't a shovel-stiff. *They* hardly notice that sort o' horse-play . . . *I* do,' he muttered dangerously.

Cuffing his hat against his arm, Cal stepped up on to the boardwalk. He watched as the men rode down the street, smiled keenly as they reined their horses in, dismounted outside a deadfall bar.

Cal walked towards them. He stopped outside for a moment, went thoughtful and then he turned in.

'Yeah, that's it,' he said quietly as he pushed at the cracked, slatted door. 'If I'm not mistaken, there's a touch of Barkdale guard about these two.'

The bar-room burned under the heat of the overhead sun. Despite the canvas sides of the structure being furled, there was no air to dissipate the fumes of grubby miners, tobacco-smoke and spilled beer.

Men were pressed to the bar, but Cal saw the two he'd come looking for, noted the arm's length of space they had around them.

He made straight towards them, but stopped when a miner brushed past him. The man's hairy face made a faltering grin.

'Frisco Gentle an' Oaky Bunns. They're lode strippers. On a bad day, they don't even say "no" to rollin' a drunk. Goddamned carrion. Stay away from 'em,' he said seriously.

Cal thanked the man, continued straight to the bar.

The man he singled out was the bearded one, wore a greasy black suit. His right hand rested on the bar, gripped a tumbler of whiskey. Cal guessed he carried a handgun under his coat.

The clean-shaven sniggerer looked up as Cal moved close.

'Looks like someone come to sell their diggins', Oaky,' he said in his shrill voice.

'No,' Cal cut in. 'I've come mail-order. I'm the "cowboy" you knocked down in the street just now. I've had a word with that dumb mule o' yours outside, but I reckon it's *you* needs his butt kicked.'

Oaky laughed, lifted his glass derisively as Cal drove his elbow in hard. The man's arm jolted and the whiskey spilled down his chin, ran into his matted beard. He cursed and turned vehemently towards Cal, dropping the glass on to the bar.

'Oops,' Cal said, grinning evilly. 'You vultures sure are clumsy birds . . . ugly too.'

Cal looked to Frisco Gentle, but it was enough for Oaky Bunns. The big man balled his right hand into a fist and lashed out angrily.

The force of the blow against Cal's forehead hurt. For a brief moment, it drove him into blackness as he fell back against the bar. He straightened his legs and held out his left hand, bolo'd his right. But it was like punching a steer and had as much effect.

'Bad move,' Bunns wheezed as he lumbered forward. 'You should o' stayed in the road.'

His fists drove into Cal's body, forcing him back again. Cal blocked some of the blows with his arms, but it was a loose guard and big, hard knuckles found their mark. Bunns piled in with rib-smashing blows and Cal's feet slipped beneath the onslaught.

He went down on to one knee, tried to hold there for a breather. But instantly Bunns took advantage. He hopped back and let drive with a boot. It was intended to crack ribs, but Cal rolled tight. He clutched the heel and pulled Bunns down to the floor. Both men cursed and spat, came up like sparring bears.

Cal was rasping air, and blood spilled from his nose. He tried to back off and get a clear thought as Bunns went into a head-down charge. Cal drove his fists with short chopping blows but Bunns looped out an arm. It thudded against the side of Cal's head and he reeled from the ferocious battering. He crashed into a card-table and toppled to the floor again, caught the glancing impact of Bunns's fists as they hammered across the back of his head and neck.

He twisted around, saw Bunns's glare of conquest. But he also saw something beyond, as the man came forward kicking. It was the other one, Frisco Gentle, who was moving shiftily away from the crowd of excited miners. Then Cal saw the man who'd spoken to him earlier. The miner thrust out an arm, clamped a big hand around the whole of the man's bald face, spectacles and all.

Great, Cal thought. The help was an encouragement, all he needed.

He rolled to one side and avoided Bunns's feet, edged into a chair. He grabbed it and held it out in front of him as Bunns surged forward.

He launched the chair up and away from him and one of its legs went into Bunns's top lip. The blood was instant and so was the pain. The big man reeled, and Cal quickly got to his feet.

Some of the miners began shouting, and Bunns raged, threw himself forward. He circled, his arms weaving, his fists pumping, trying to smash Cal. But Cal kept his distance, was getting the better of the bigger man. He took a small step back and feinted, measured out one good punch. He went forward, put his weight behind a straight-armed drive with his right hand. He felt the jar

69

deep into his shoulder as the blow connected with the front of Bunns's bloodied face.

The man's eyes lost their rage then, took on a drowsy glaze. His legs made a strange stiff wobble, and Cal hit him again. He didn't move his feet and kept his left arm down at his side. He threw another right, then more, each one short and precise. Bunns's head fell and Cal lifted it each time on the end of his fist, felt the pain and warm slush from his punches. Bunns crumpled to the floor gurgling, clawing at the wet and dirt, his body quivering as he tried to bring himself up again. Cal wiped the man's blood and mucous from his fingers, turned to face the other man.

The miner ungripped Frisco Gentle's head and Cal nodded.

'Someone get 'em out of here ... before they get hurt,' he said, breathing heavily. He licked drily at his lips and turned to the bar. Groups of men were grinning, animatedly discussing the scrap, and one of them pushed a schooner of beer at him.

The miner who'd warned him earlier thrust out a hand the size of a shovel.

'I could've done with one o' those myself,' Cal said, and almost smiled.

'You did good, feller, an' you can forget about Bunns,' the miner advised. 'It's Frisco Gentle who's the wretched one. Yessir, a real backshooter. He walks ahead, if you know what I mean?'

Cal nodded appreciatively. 'I'll try an' remember that,' he said.

'What's your name, mister?' the miner then asked.

Cal took a long gulp of the beer he'd been handed before he answered.

'Calvin Crow.'

'I'm Pug Edgcumbe. Call me Pug. You come to Sego lookin' to get rich, Mr Crow?'

'Let's say I'm driftin' with anticipation,' Cal said enigmatically.

Edgcumbe laughed gently. 'Yeah, ain't we all,' he said. 'Maybe I can help you out,' he added after a short silence. 'There's a small, likely seam that forks off my claim. It's yours if you want to make somethin' of it.'

Cal set his beer on the counter, looked directly at Edgcumbe. His voice was flat, carried no leaning.

'Why would you want to make such an offer? Any claim on the north face must be worth a heap o' money?'

Edgcumbe banged his own beer-glass down on the counter.

'Hell, man, you're the best entertainment ever visited this town. My guess is there's more to come, an' I'm investin' in it. But you're right about the claim, so I ain't beggin' you to take it, Mr Crow.'

Cal turned away, stared at the mantel clock behind the bar, took a sip of his beer.

Pug Edgcumbe knew Cal was weighing up the situation, the offer, and he moved off a pace, stood quietly waiting for an answer.

For Cal, the bouts of violence were rasping away his restiveness. Maybe he was getting too old, too tired for the fight. It would have to end sometime, the memory of his boy's last words, the look on his face. How many men would he be ready to thump, kill even, because of Krewel and Gibson? How many more weeks, months, maybe years of a gruelling obsession? Perhaps he could end the trail in Sego Bench; forget Barkdale; try and put young Walker from his mind for good.

He could make *some* of it happen . . . and if he ever did meet up with Krewel or Gibson . . . well! He shook his head, turned to Edgcumbe.

'I'm impressed by how much you're prepared to pay for me to amuse you. I hope you don't want another chorus . . . not just yet.' Cal offered his hand to Edgcumbe. 'And if you mean it about that seam . . . maybe I could stay around a while longer,' he added with a slow, dry smile.

Edgcumbe was pleased. He'd played his part, done his bit by Lauren Garth. He didn't think it would harm his standing.

# 9
# Staking a Claim

Two hours later, Calvin Crow left town in Pug Edgcumbe's mud-wagon. From the north end of Sego Bench, they followed the deeply rutted road along San Simon Creek, past countless miners beavering away at their claim-washing. Occasionally a man would raise his head and shout a familiar greeting to Edgcumbe, who'd roar something appropriate back.

'Reckon this water's pegged out right up to the Gila,' he said to Cal. 'To some of 'em, paddlin' in the creek's more important than diggin' for blue stuff.' Pug had a chaw of Brown Mule, paused for a moment to squirt its juice into the road. 'Me, I'd be figgerin' a way to bring water to the claim. You should think on that, Cal. Maybe if we run a chute down, we can both use it.'

'Yeah,' Cal said, almost inattentively. He was looking suspiciously at the face of every man they passed. Over many months it had become second nature to him, but if Pug noticed, he thought better than to mention it.

After the road forded the shallow creek, the two men climbed from the wagon and loose-hobbled the mule.

They took a path that verged the rocky walls of the creek, walked for nearly a half-mile to where the path opened on to a silty bank. A few old army tents were closely grouped, but Pug led them past, into what was becoming a narrow canyon. Across the rippling creek-bed Cal stopped to look at the soft clay that held skim-diggings along the water's edge.

'Soft bed, soft in the head,' Pug scoffed. 'They're in such a goddamned panic to find the ore, they're stampin' most of it into the mud. I've probably riddled a full poke from what they've pissed on.' He spat to the ground, pointed across to a can-chimneyed shanty.

'Home. The seams're a hundred yards on . . . beyond the piñon.'

Cal stared ahead, could see a shadowy tear in the arroyo wall. The nut pine ran close to the opening, and the two men had to push their way through mesquite and broom.

Cal's seam ran for nearly fifty yards, then shafted upward to the skyline.

'All o' this section falls in the San Simon Territory,' Pug said. 'In Sego we got ourselves a claims recorder an' an agency. We had a sheriff for a while, but Oaky Bunns sent him across the plateau. No one's been too keen to apply for the job since.'

'What part do you play in all this?' Cal asked.

'Agency chairman,' Pug answered, and winked. 'Anyways, we don't need a sheriff. We got laws and most abide by 'em. There's always some as forgets, but we make out.'

Cal folded his arms, surveyed the land.

'Which o' them laws affects me?' he asked.

'Work your claim within ten days of stakin' it out. This is a gulch claim, so from where we're standin' it's thirty-three paces up the bed.'

'How wide?'

Pug, spread his arms.

'Side to side. A spade length on top o' that for your boundary markers.'

'Hmmm,' Cal considered. 'Then I record it in town, I suppose?'

'Yep. Then all you gotta do is keep your eyes open an' dig.'

Cal nodded slow and thoughtful.

'What you goin' to do, Pug?' he asked.

'I've just about had my time, Cal. Another two months, then I'll call it a day. Get myself home before winter sets in.'

'Where's that?'

'Great Bend . . . a day's ride north-west o' Wichita.'

'That's a hell of a wagon-ride. I wish you luck, Pug, an' thanks.'

'Yeah,' Pug said, and spat against a rock. 'Remember no amount o' money's worth dyin' for, Cal. You gotta get to spend it . . . at least some of it.'

Twenty minutes later Cal watched Pug Edgcumbe turn and wave as he disappeared through the mesquite at the entrance to the gulch.

Cal turned around and stared at the rugged walls, the small outcrops of slick-rock and grass. He'd made his decision, but having a silver-mine wasn't as immediately exciting as he'd thought it would be. He sniffed indifferently, thought what the hell. He moved on up the gulch, contemplated what would have happened if he'd taken on the small hairless man as well as Oaky Bunns. Conceivably Pug would have paid for supplies. He was going to need a good tarp, bedding and tools to work his claim.

He started to pace off, counted to thirty and kicked up a rock, heaped a low pile around it. Then he crossed the gulch and built up a similar mound, did what Pug told him and placed his name and date amongst the stones. That was a significant deed and he sat awhile. His shoulder hurt him, from the fight with Bunns, but he felt satisfied at having marked some ground. He looked along the claim, squinted up at the skyline.

The day's shadows were lengthening when Cal decided where he'd make his cabin. It would be set back from the entrance to the gulch in the lee of a stunted oak. He couldn't do much about it being overlooked, but it would be where he'd start digging for the blue stuff.

It was early dark when Cal returned to Sego Bench and the town was already well into its evening hullabaloo. He'd arrived with maybe fifty other miners, and for the first time he had to queue to file his claim with the camp recorder. When that was completed, he went to the tented grub-house for his supper, went through the menu with beef, beans and coffee.

He passed Black Jack's, and noticed the sign had been taken down, saw the new one. The words were painted in red, with yellow and gold flourishes.

THE ARIZONA ROSE, it said. Standing underneath it, with his hands pushed deep in his pockets and looking well satisfied, was Franklin Henner. He saw Cal approaching.

'Where in tarnation you been?' he greeted him. 'I

been real worried about you.'

'Yeah, an' bears have stopped crappin' in the woods,' Cal retorted. 'Somebody offered me a claim. It's not much more than a one-holer, but I thought I'd give it a go.' Cal looked up, nodded at the new sign. 'How 'bout you? Looks like you been busy.'

'An inch o' time is an inch o' gold. Or in this case, silver. I too had a bit o' luck,' Henner said, and smiled broadly.

Cal listened to the industrious hum from inside the building, shook his head.

'I'd say you're goin' to make your first dollar ahead o' me, Frank.'

Henner thought for a moment, took his hands from his pockets.

'I'll need to. These improvements have cost me all the money I've ever had,' he said. He thought for a moment, winked shrewdly. 'We could make that "first dollar" together, Cal. You have . . . let's say . . . certain management skills, which would be useful to me.'

'I can't work indoors, Frank . . . never could. But if I ever change my mind, you'll be the first to know.'

Henner shrugged. 'I know you well enough not to argue, but Miss Lauren's come in with me. If that makes a difference?'

'No it don't. Miss Lauren's never worked anywhere else *but* indoors.' Cal looked again at the saloon, the carpenters hammering away at the improvements. 'Each to one's own,' he said.

There was a new-found purpose to Henner's outlook, and he wasn't going to waste any real time on finding a third partner.

'Lauren did ask if I'd seen you,' he mentioned.

Cal creased up his brow, looked a little uncomfortable.

'Then tell her you did,' he said more cold-heartedly than he felt. He raised his hand in farewell and crossed the street, aware that Henner was looking after him bemusedly.

He went into Ellwood's Variety Store. It was another weather-beaten structure, but one of the few with the lavishness of window-glass across the front. The interior was a vast clutter of goods, stacked and piled all over. Alongside the day-by-day supplies, there was everything rich and reckless miners might need in the way of glamorous foods: turtle-soup, hams, dried fruits, even Chinese delicacies. All of it had been hauled in from Las Cruces where, in turn, it had been carted from the railhead at El Paso.

Cal purchased an axe, pick, shovel, and a pan to wash his mud. Two lanterns and a gallon of coal oil cost him five dollars. A buffalo-hide and a week's supply of plain foodstuffs finished his order and even without the $10 a bottle Champagne, the total almost cleaned him out.

Grudgingly, he paid the bill.

'I'll collect all this later,' he told the shopkeeper. 'When do you close?'

The aproned man looked Cal over.

'When business stops comin' in,' he said. 'That'll most likely be after midnight.'

Cal was impressed, whistled sharply through his teeth. He went outside, had a look up and down the street. A steady stream of men were coursing into the San Simon, most of them from the old worked-out Comstock and Arizona Territory mines. Mule- and ox-teams, groaning ore-wagons and sturdy carts moved non-stop with food-stuffs and hardware. Wood was stacked along the street, outside half-built stores, offices and more saloons. Oil-lamps lined the boardwalks, flared into the night to keep the workmen busy in their effort to build another crate city.

A rowdy fist-fight broke out, was broken up by a mob of longhorns. The cattle were being driven into town to taunt the miners with fresh meat, find the highest bidder. Cal turned to see Franklin Henner waving from outside his saloon.

'I'll double your best offer. Come back an' ask for Frank Henner,' he shouted at the cowboy riding herd.

Cal had a quiet laugh and watched the cattle pass, walked further down the street. He saw Chubby Pound shambling towards him.

'Buy you a drink?' Cal offered. 'I've probably got enough for a bottle between us.'

Chubby considered Cal's offer. 'Yeah, thanks,' he said.

He followed Cal along to the Arizona Rose where lamps lighted the building's front which had been scrubbed clean. From inside came the spiky hammering of a piano, then they heard the incongruous, but pleas-ing, tones of a woman singing.

Cal pushed through the swing-doors, was immediately cut by the smell of fresh paint that mingled with the sweat and beer. Smoke hung low, curled lazily across the room and men stood crushed against the long bar.

At one end of the room, a stage had been hurriedly raised. It was made of shore-planking nailed to heavy cross-tree supports. Six ornate reflector lamps had been fixed along the front, and in the flood of light stood the young woman. She wore a red, sparkly dress that broke up the light into a thousand stars, some of it across the strained, dark faces of the miners.

All the men had been captivated by the song. She was singing a bittersweet melody and it produced an unnerving melancholy.

Chubby Pound winked at Cal, sniffed audibly and cursed.

'I'm a durned corny old fool,' he said. 'I must o' heard that song a hundred times an' still get a run in my nose.'

Cal stood watching the girl. 'You're meant to, you old goat,' he said good-naturedly. 'The girl's an expert worker.'

The singer kept her eyes closed while she finished the song. A long moment after the final note, when the applause had died down, Lauren Garth looked around her and smiled happily.

A man close to the stage called out.

'Give us *Dancin' Britches* Lauren.'

Lauren threw her head back and laughed.

'You'll get them all, fellers. Just give me time to get my breath an' a drink. I ain't goin' nowhere.'

Pleased at having teamed up with his coaching friends again, Chubby Pound used his considerable weight, elbowed his way enthusiastically up to the bar. His big, round face was beaming.

'Goddamnit, Cal. I betcha Miss Lauren don't get run out o' *this* town.'

'I hope none of us does,' Cal said drily.

He turned back to the stage but Lauren was gone. The piano-player was pounding out a popular dance-tune and some of the miners were dancing with each other, stomping and whirling excitedly.

The bartender got down the line and set up a bottle and two glass tumblers. Chubby shivered involuntarily as he grabbed the bottle and poured.

'Thanks Cal, you're all right. I'm lookin' forward to this,' he said. He made a painful sound as he swallowed the whiskey. He refilled his glass and handed Cal the bottle.

A man standing behind them said, 'Miss Lauren, I'm buyin' you a drink.'

Lauren took no notice. She was looking at Cal as she stepped close. The look on her face had changed to serious.

'Have you found what you were lookin' for?' she asked, raising her voice above the noise.

Cal bit his lip, thought, then spoke slowly.

'I'm not sure. I've staked out a claim along the creek aways. I guess I'll be stayin' in Sego 'til I know the answer to that question.' He looked into her eyes. 'The Arizona Rose, eh? You never told me you could sing. You've hidden depths, Lauren.'

Cal saw surprise in her face, saw it disappear.

'I'll bring 'em to the surface,' she said, smiling sadly. 'You'll be passing through then?'

'Yes, Lauren. I'll be passing through. Might even pass through here.'

She gave him a long expressive look, then turned away. Cal carefully placed his empty glass on the bar and Chubby grinned.

'Don't often see that . . . not real close up,' he said. 'To most of us, a girl like that we have to pay handsome.

But to *you* . . . well . . .' Chubby broke off and blew on his fingertips, whistled a couple of flat notes.

Cal smiled, had a look around him, then left the saloon. Chubby set off for the grub-house and Cal went back to the store. He picked up his supplies and set out for the arroyo and his claim.

# 10
# Line of Command

Jared Munroe stood at the bar of the Long Lizard saloon, used his last dollar to pay for his drink.

'Goddamn peakers,' he muttered, looking around him at the itinerant miners.

The San Simon lodes were beginning to look rich, but it had been a few years since he'd tried his luck in the fields, blistered his hands on the haft of a pick. No matter how bad things were, he wasn't prepared to join them just yet.

Munroe had spent most of his life in south Texas, and the fact he could never return was his only claim to fame. From the West Nueces to Houston there would be a rope waiting for him, and a big handful of ranchers eager to slap the pony. He'd burned a lot of boats, and now wondered about the cattle trade in Utah or Nevada.

The glass of busthead whiskey carried out its usual and immediate assault inside him and for a while he felt safe, took comfort from his anonymity in the boisterous surroundings.

Then, from a reflection in the back-bar mirror, he

became aware of the small, beardless man who wore spectacles. The man was staring at him with certain interest and for a moment it troubled Munroe's mood. He sucked at the glass and wiped the back of his hand across his mouth. Then he turned from the bar and with calculated shakiness walked from the building.

Out on the boardwalk he paused, took a couple of deep breaths. The sharp air freed up his head, but he put a sway and a random stagger into his walk as he made his way down the street. He stopped outside a freighters' depot, held both hands against the window. He had a furtive glance at the man following him, saw another one. It was a bigger man, heavily bearded and wearing a dark suit. Munroe smirked, spoke drunkenly to the window and moved on.

He reeled against a few more buildings, then staggered awkwardly into the stub alley alongside Bernie's Bar. Within seconds he heard a voice calling in the darkness.

'For Chrissakes, Oaky, where's he gone? Find him.'

The pretend drunkeness gone, Munroe pushed his back hard against one of the sidewalls in the alley. He pulled the big revolver, held it beside him, ready to swing up and round.

The bigger of the two men who'd been following him ran pell-mell into the dark lane, exhaled noisily, cursed as the barrel of the gun stabbed violently into his low-slung gut.

'If you're Oaky, tell that weasel to join us here,' Munroe whispered. 'Anythin' else . . . get ready for the pain.'

Oaky Bunns responded to the threat, the shadowy set of Munroe's face.

'In here, Frisco,' he said shakily.

Almost immediately, Frisco Gentle turned into the alley.

'What the hell you doin' Oaky? I told you ...' his high-pitched voice demanded, breaking off as Munroe's left hand grabbed his coat-sleeve, swung him down to his knees.

'You dirty high-graders,' Munroe rasped at them. 'You won't be relievin' me of any ore-bag.'

'It's this hogleg that makes *you* so law abidin' is it then?' Bunns growled.

'Right now, you're goddamned right it is,' Munroe snapped. He took a step back, and swung the barrel hard into Bunns's mouth. The face made a dull, shattering sound as the man sank to his knees alongside Gentle.

'Our mistake, an' Oaky ain't ever gonna learn,' Frisco Gentle said quickly. He lifted his hands and cowered from Munroe, his usual, thin sniggering suddenly silent.

'Oh, he will, friend ... he will,' Munroe disagreed. 'And so will you.'

Gentle moved his knees in the dirt, edged away from Bunns.

'I know you from somewhere else,' he said. 'Uvalde ... bumpin' cattle along the Nueces Strip.'

'Yeah, well I been around. What of it?' Munroe challenged.

'The currency here's blue ore, friend. You can forget them owl-hoot tricks. Anyways, this territory's already been marked.'

Munroe snarled at him. 'What gibberish is that?'

'Your speciality ain't needed here. The inn's full. Do you understand *that*?' Gentle continued with a degree of nerve. 'I found out the hard way. Oaky here . . . he's still learnin'. You'll be doin' the same, unless you find a new use for that beef-head cunning.'

Oaky Bunns growled painfully as he hauled himself up. He spread his hands against the wall of the building to hold himself steady.

'You'll live, Oaky,' Gentle said, as he too got to his feet. 'Lucky it's your head what's takin' the worst.'

Bunns glared at Munroe. He started to say something, but the words wouldn't come.

Gentle spoke up again. 'Look feller,' he said to Munroe, 'you're ahead at the moment, but if you go upsettin' the peckin' order o' this town, you're dead meat.'

Munroe snorted his contempt. 'Shut your prattlin' and move on . . . both o' you, before I turn nasty. I'm getting tired o' your distraction.'

Gentle brushed dirt from his knees, wrung his hands schemingly.

'Maybe I could distract you for a drink. Distract you with a no-risk, get-rich proposal.'

Munroe slipped the revolver into his holster, weighed up the man silently.

Gentle's high-pitched, cackly laughter returned.

'I reckon you should be real interested,' he said. 'We'll get back to the Lizard . . . start over . . . no hard feelins'. Later on, we're meetin' someone. Hang around.'

Munroe laughed. 'You were beginnin' to sound like one o' them Eastern salesmen,' he said. 'Still, what the hell. You or the griz pull a fast one, and you'll be the dead meat.'

The three men walked back along the street. Intuition told Munroe to let Gentle walk ahead; Bunns did it naturally. They returned to the Long Lizard and Gentle set up the whiskies. Bunns had a difficult word with one of the barkeeps, accepted a cloth to dab at his wounded face.

Frisco Gentle seemed oblivious to the hostility his presence created at the bar. He made casual conversation for a while, but Munroe's caution and lack of response finally closed him down. He refilled their glasses and eventually Munroe let him pay for the bottle.

Oaky Bunns came and stood between them. Sensing Calvin Crow might be present, he looked around the bar.

'I don't like this, Frisco,' he mumbled awkwardly. 'Don't feel good.'

'No, I don't suppose you do,' Gentle said unemotionally. He thumbed open a pocket watch. 'It's nearly midnight, anyway. Let's get out of here,' he suggested to Munroe.

The men walked out into the late hurly-burly of the street.

'Let's go meet a man,' Gentle said, then walked off without saying another word.

Gentle led them nearly a half-mile beyond the town limits. He turned off the roadway along a rough trail to where pale yellow lamplight glowed in the open windows of a big miners' cabin. From deep in a stand of nut-pine they heard the unmistakable whinny of a horse.

'That's his big claybank,' Bunns said. 'If he's been waitin', he'll chew us up, Frisco.'

'Can it, Oaky! Just let me do the talkin', you hear?'

Frisco turned his pale, sharp face towards Munroe. 'You'll be wise to listen up too.'

Gentle rapped twice on the door, and took a step back. When the door opened, a shadowy figure appeared, asked who was there.

'Frisco,' Gentle answered decisively. 'There's three of us.'

The door swung inwards, and a wedge of light fell across the stony ground.

'Is he here?' Gentle asked.

The man shut the door behind them before he replied.

'Yeah. *He's* here. *You* took your time, though.'

Gentle snorted, pushed his way in and Munroe followed, blinking at the rich, pungent atmosphere. Four lanterns burned in a line overhead and the room seemed to be crammed with other men, but Munroe quickly counted eight. All of them were using tobacco, either chewing or smoking it. They had been talking, but stopped to eye up Gentle and his company.

The man who'd opened the door went to the back of the cabin, poked his head in a smaller room. In the quiet, they could hear him speaking to someone.

'They're all in, boss.'

Munroe immediately felt ill at ease. He began to sweat when he realized that none of the men appeared to be miners or town workmen. He eased his hand beneath his coat, rested his palm on the butt of the big revolver.

A tall figure stepped into the room, his pale eyes hunting out the seated men. The man looked through Munroe, but it was only a moment before Marshal Denton Lome cracked a thin smile.

'Well, if it ain't the cow thief,' he said in his hard voice. 'I thought you'd turn up sooner or later.'

Munroe's blood-pressure rose, and his heart thumped. He didn't say anything, didn't trust the tenor of his voice. He nodded weakly, and after an unnerving moment Lome's interest moved on.

'Some of you know me from Las Cruces,' he said. 'Some from Denning. But you *all* know of my word. I can give you protection from a night in the cooler or a hangin', even.'

Lome used the hush, his authority to concentrate the minds of the gathered men.

'But there's somethin' off-beam with breakin' the law. You'll have a bastard like me on your trail,' he continued, enjoying the menace. 'Out here, the nearest oak will satisfy any miners' court.'

Munroe took a deep breath. And swore silently, wondered exactly who was going to end up as the dead meat.

Lome caught his eye, seemed to read his thoughts.

'I'm here to tell you, that ain't gonna happen. Not if you listen good.' Lome smiled complacently. 'The cow-thief here, ain't ever worked with any of us. But he will, if he don't wanna be hemp-fodder. Get yourselves organized an' San Simon'll give up a bigger lode than the Comstock . . . an' without the diggin'.'

For a short while Lome allowed the men to exchange clannish asides, partake of a spit and a puff, then he started in again.

'Like you, I want the good stuff. This badge don't do that, it just gives me a start. What you fellers gotta remember is that I'll break heads to get what I want, an' it's too late to back away.'

Again, Lome flicked a significant glance at Munroe.

'So, we'll help each other. Your part is to keep your eyes open, work the whole creek. Be everywhere. Get your notice in, but keep your traps shut. If there's any complaints, I'll take care of 'em. If I've got anythin' to say, you'll hear of it. Remember I get *very* red-rumped, and mine's the only side I'm on.'

Lome's manner was cold and direct and Munroe wondered what the hell he'd got himself into. He knew he was in too deep to get out, shivered at the prospect ahead.

'For the time bein' I'm gonna stay in Las Cruces,' Lome said. 'That's where the state's appointin' from, an' I'm up for the San Simon Territory. When I get the office, I'll run it as a sheriff should . . . tight. I won't stand for no independent law, no goddamn *Agencies*.'

Lome stood tall, pulled on his long moustachios.

'You men will leave separately. Frisco, I want you to hitch up for a while longer,' he commanded.

As the men in the room moved off, they all looked at Munroe. He was the gringo but nothing was said, no introductions offered on either side. Munroe knew that his face was being remembered, but Lome's acceptance of him seemed to be enough. When just five of them remained, Lome spoke again.

'Hamey, go an' see my horse is all right,' he said to the man who'd opened the door. 'I'm trustin' Lyle Roach's got a bed waitin' for me in Sego.'

Oaky Bunns made restive noises, and it drew Lome's attention. The big marshal swung his hand, smacked it hard and loud across Bunns's face. Bunns staggered back with the force, but made no effort to retaliate. Munroe smelled the fear, thought Bunns was getting himself a real hard time.

Lome's face remained impassive.

'In case you're wonderin', that's for lettin' that knife man Crow, do you over,' he said. 'Think yourself lucky he didn't wanna shave you. I've told you, the man's trouble, an' I'll indulge none of it. Don't let it happen again.'

Gentle shook his head. 'Weren't Oaky's fault, Marshal,' he lied. 'I saw Crow jump him. You're right about him bein' trouble an' all. He's one dangerous dude. But I'll take care o' him . . . see it don't happen again.'

Munroe was listening with interest. Calvin Crow wasn't his friend, but didn't appear to be much of an enemy either.

'Yeah, maybe you will,' Lome muttered. He was going to say something else on the subject, but stopped. He turned to Munroe instead, spoke as if he'd been reading his mind.

'I don't normally go for the convention of knowin' names,' he said. 'But in your case I'm makin' an exception.'

'It's Munroe. Jared Munroe.'

'Last name's enough. I ain't gonna marry you,' Lome mocked. 'You're in with *us* now, whether you like it or not. You know too much not to be.' The Las Cruces lawman turned as he went out the door. 'Frisco'll tell you what to do. Just make sure you do it,' he advised gravely.

A minute later Hamey Barge returned.

'Likes to keep it near the knuckle, does the marshal,' he chortled, without looking at anyone.

'I can take that,' Munroe said, 'but right now, I got to find me somewhere to bed down.'

Gentle was watching his partner, Oaky Bunns. The dark-suited man was sitting down, holding both hands to his face.

'God damn him,' he said. 'My head ain't built to take this sort a punishment.'

'Punishment's close to guilt, Oaky. Now listen,' Gentle said sharply. 'Munroe is gonna stay with us. You just stay away from him, understand?'

Bunns glared at Munroe.

'Aagh, to hell with you all.' Bunns almost spat the words. He turned and stomped from the cabin.

Gentle gave one of his shrill wicked laughs, his small, smooth face agleam under the lamplight.

'Oaky's used to bein' beaten. He'll get roostered in a bar somewhere, and he'll be a big pussy-cat again . . . you'll see.'

Munroe grinned. 'I don't give a goddamn either way.' Then he looked slyly at Gentle. 'I've heard a lot o' talk this night. When do we see somethin' for it?'

Gentle returned the grin, lifted a parting hand to Barge.

'Be patient, it'll happen,' he said. 'Let's make tracks.'

# 11
# Gentle Warning

Calvin Crow swung his axe at pine that topped the surrounding ridge. He kicked the felled timber down to the gulch floor, used it to construct the walls of his cabin. On a stretched-out tarp he smeared brea to make a water resistant roof. He cut larch poles and made a cot frame, stuffed bunch grass into gunny sacks for his mattress.

He usually worked from first to last light, and when he eventually stood in his doorway and looked around him, he was brimming with achievement. He went inside and sat on a pile of log ends, ate canned food off his big-bladed knife. He sliced at bully-beef, and speared peaches, pushing them into his mouth, whole. He boiled strong coffee, happily spooned in milk and sugar. At some time, he thought he might buy a handgun from Ellwood's, maybe find himself a dog to share the adventure with.

The moon had risen and, in the deep, embracing, night silence, Cal heard the crush of pine blowdown. It was Pug Edgcumbe approaching the cabin.

Still holding his knife, Cal got to his feet. The miner stepped up to the doorway, grinned at him.

'Mighty fine,' he said, looking at the rude interior. He perched himself on the wood-pile and Cal poured some coffee into an empty food-can, blinked at the sweetness.

'Oh yes, mighty fine,' he repeated slowly, with feeling.

Cal put a match to another jack lamp, listened as Pug advised him.

'You can run a claim assessment tomorrow. Try both sides of the gulch, and look for low layers under the oxides. Sometimes you can find them where water's bruised the boulder rock. Split 'em apart an' let the silver run.'

'Thanks Pug, I'll do just that.' Cal was thoughtful, his mind going over the routine.

Pug looked at him, oddly.

'Strange thing about towns like Sego Bench,' he said. 'The way a rumour touches everyone. It's like a bad smell . . . only it lasts a mite longer . . . picks up weight.' Pug's brow creased. 'Word's gone out that you're bein' pecked by Oaky Bunns an' Frisco Gentle. I don't suppose you'd put much store in that, Cal . . . with the fight an' all. But just remember, some o' them stone mounds can become more'n boundary markers.'

Cal scowled. 'Them two are less trouble than gettin' boots to fit.'

'Yeah, I'm sure they are Cal. But the San Simon's gonna be a real big strike. I know it. There won't be just miners that come to Sego Bench. There'll be more like Bunns an' Gentle. The town'll fill with every sinner known to Christendom, and then some. And with them, come the claim-jumpers an' backshooters.' Pug walked to the doorway, tossed the dregs of his coffee out. 'I've seen it happen before,' he continued. 'I was in Nevada.

94

Never struck more'n worms, but I saw what happened to many that did.'

'What are you tryin' to tell me, Pug? I recall it was you wanted me to work the claim.'

'Yeah, I did . . . I do. But maybe I got it wrong. There are some of us here who mean to see there's no trouble . . . no real trouble. But now I don't know, Cal.'

Pug stared into the darkness of the gulch.

'Other than strikin' a blue deposit, most o' the miners along the San Simon have an undemandin' outlook on life. They'll soak up a lot before they get to be fightin' mad. They all figure they'll make it one day, an' go home rich. But most of 'em never will. Scum like Frisco Gentle trade on that. If the miners ever get wrecked, the creek'll run red.'

'I can take care o' myself Pug. Don't be troubled over me,' Cal said quietly.

Pug turned and looked sharply at him.

'Bunns will want to get at you, but it's the mean one, Gentle, who'll take his time. You're your own man, Cal, and it frightens 'em. You're a threat to their authority, an' they'll try an' take you out . . . believe me.'

Cal sounded concerned. 'But you won't let 'em, right? You have an outfit to take care o' that sort o' thing?'

Pug nodded. 'Yeah, that's right. You won't be on your own, but we ain't got any real law to back us, remember. Let's hope that together we can put the frighteners on that pair o' wasps.'

Cal hefted the big Green River knife. 'They got one o' them new Frontier Colts in Ellwood's. When I fill my first poke, reckon I'll buy me one.'

'Well, we can all sleep easy in our beds knowin' that,'

95

Pug said, cheerfully. 'Perhaps I'll see somethin' of you tomorrow. Get some sleep.'

In the moonlight, Cal watched the shadow of his friend weave through the gulch, through the tangle of mesquite and broom, back to the creek.

An hour after Pug had gone, Cal rolled into his buffalo hide. But he was too tired to sleep; there were too many thoughts inside his head. Without much effort, wanton thoughts of Lauren Garth gripped him. He made a wry smile in the darkness. Perhaps at last someone else was winning the battle of his dreams. He stared up at his roof, hoped he wouldn't be under the first snows.

Five hours later, Cal ran his claim assessment. He dug along the bottom line, up the gulch sides looking for seam traces. He worked methodically, slicing layers from the silty ground, heaping the residue on to the bankside shingle. He quit at noon and burned some greasewood stumps outside his cabin, ate some more beef, reheated his coffee-can.

When he returned to the digging section, he carried a pail and a panning-tray. He went to where he'd left off, then worked his way back. He shovelled a gallon of deposits into the pail, then made his way out of the gulch, along the creek towards Pug Edgcumbe's cabin.

The egg-sized stones hurt the soles of his feet, and after twenty minutes the coldness chilled his fingers and the backs of his legs. Standing in the creek, Cal swirled the pan, washed the dirt. He flicked from the rim of the pan, retained the black sand. There were oxide traces, but, to Cal's eye, nothing much more.

Before he'd finished working his third pan, Pug was at

the creek-side. Cal showed him the grainy contents, and he laughed.

'Should be enough to stand you a small beer. Let's see if two of us can make any difference,' he said.

Pug had brought a long pan, and, together, they quickly worked their way through the remainder of the deposit. They fared better towards the bottom of the pail, panned out nearly a dollar's worth of grain silver.

'Gettin' richer as you move up the seam, that's obvious,' Pug explained.

The yield from the next four buckets was even higher, and it got to first dark before Cal collapsed exhausted on the bank. It was only a beginning but, in eight hours, he'd tipped maybe fifteen dollars of blue grain into his flattened peach can.

Pug had gone to work his own claim, but it was nearby and he kept an eye on Cal's activity.

'Looks promisin'. Maybe I'm workin' the wrong claim after all,' he called out as he approached. 'But you'll need a more accommodatin' rig than a slops bucket. Get yourself a hand-barrow.'

Cal stared wistfully at his pail.

'I'll go into town . . . get the blacksmith to nail some wheels on it,' he said, and both men laughed.

After dark, Cal thought about what Pug had suggested and made his way into Sego Bench. It was late, but the main street was seething. In the light from the boardwalk lamps, steam curled around sweating animals as they hauled mining gear in and out of town.

The strikes along the north slopes had certainly brought the men. They'd come on the run, unprepared and raring to go. Cal knew most of them would be disappointed. Very few would make a profit, let alone strike it rich. Most of them could have stayed at home, made more money from farm or store work.

At Ellwood's Variety Store, Cal bought a hand-cart and a leather drawstring pouch. Into it, he poured his day's tailings from the peach can, used some of the grain as payment. It was a simple transaction, but to him, a new and gratifying experience.

Back in the street it was full night and Cal looked twice at the bright, enticing lights of the Arizona Rose, shook his head and walked on. The miners worked non-stop. They even had tar flares attached to the sides of their wagons. Alongside the Stack saloon, near the man who was selling shovels, someone had set up a lean-to stall. A hanging poster simply proclaimed: MEAT AND OTHER FOODSTUFFS. HOGBACK $5 A POUND

Cal smiled at the 'other foodstuffs'. He bought two thick bacon slices, used up a few more grains.

The storekeeper grinned. 'You making good?' he asked.

Cal shook his head. 'Naagh. This is a long day's money, I'm spendin'. But you never know, an' it's still more'n a puncher makes.'

The man laughed, handed over the meat.

Alongside the creek, away from the town, the glow of a lantern in Pug Edgcumbe's shanty glowed welcomingly. It lit the pitch-blackness of the gulch, and Cal walked towards it.

Pug was banging hobnails into the sole of a boot when Cal arrived, brandishing the bacon slices.

He got up and whistled appreciatively.

'Welcome, feller,' he said. 'That looks mighty welcome. Where'd you get it?'

'Cut it from Oaky Bunns's belly.'

Pug shook his head in a friendly, exasperated manner, laid the long mining-pan on the glowing embers of his fire. Fifteen minutes on, they ate the fried crispy meat with tinned peas and *frijoles*, and in near total silence.

When they'd finished Pug put his feet up on a flour barrel, sorted out a chaw of his Brown Mule.

Cal enjoyed the camaraderie, but a part of him felt uneasy, didn't fully appreciate the minute. Because of the Barkdale pen it had been a long time since he'd been alone with another man without thoughts of retribution and killing. But things were turning out differently now, and he made quiet acceptance of Pug's simple friendship.

After a few minutes Pug grinned long-sufferingly.

'I sometimes wonder if it's worth puttin' in another day in this god-forsaken hole,' he said. 'Tryin' to stay alive. Afeared of everythin' that moves, an' most that don't. Meltin' our skins for a trace o' blue stuff, when what we really need is home comforts.'

'Yeah. I've been thinkin' over what you were tellin' me yesterday,' Cal said.

'Talk and look poor. Stay quiet an' stay breathin'.'

'Mmmm,' Cal mused. 'You won't be talkin' poor when you get back to . . . where was it . . . Kansas someplace?'

'Yeah, Great Bend. In a few weeks' time I'm gonna climb that ridge above your cabin, cut me a pine. I'll drag it all the way home if I have to. Them kids o' mine can have a real Christmas tree.'

'What else you want Pug?'

'One o' them fringe-top surreys, to drive the whole family to church on Sundays. I'll get Essie some new dresses, an' me a big bag o' doodads . . . a lotta things I don't need. Some dreams maybe . . . no more blowin' out the lamps at night.' Pug laughed, then went thoughtful before he questioned Cal.

'How about you, Cal? What's your reason for bein' here?'

Cal was caught off guard. For a moment he paused, then shook his head slowly.

'I don't have much of a reason for bein' anywhere, Pug. That's the hell of it,' he lied. 'It's a long story an' much of it ain't for the tellin' now.'

Pug sensed the underlying anguish, decided to leave things as they were.

For Cal, the warmth of the night bled away. Once again, the sense of unfinished business reared itself, the revenge. It hadn't gone away.

Back at his own cabin, Cal recalled what Pug had said about being rich enough to burn oil through the night.

'Yeah, that's me, pardner,' he said acidly, and turned his lamp up, rolled into the musty comfort of the buffalo hide.

For a long hour he mentally ticked off the things he could do to get himself more settled; the stock he'd need to purchase from Ellwood's, the building-timber he'd need to cut. He was thinking of Pug's idea for a water spillway and rocker, wrestling with the problem of how to keep going, when he fell asleep.

Cal heard the sharp report, wondered about the dull,

far away sound in his head. As he woke, something smashed into the door of his cabin.

'Judas Priest,' he yelled, rolling to the floor. 'I was right, goddamnit. I'm goin' beaver.'

The heavy-calibre rifle-shot came from the ridge, he reflected angrily. Even as he attempted to extinguish his lamp, another bullet took out his flimsy window-shutter. It struck a pan-handle, ricocheted up through the roof-tarp.

# 12
# $1,000 Lode

Cal lay full length beside his cot. If he got up to extinguish the lamp he'd probably get shot. If he knocked it out, it would spill and set fire to the cabin. He swore again. If he'd thought about being ambushed, it stood to reason that somebody else would. Pug had even warned him of the 'claim-jumpers and backshooters'.

He dragged on his boots, thought quickly. If he tried to leave, the rifleman would see him come through the door. He'd be silhouetted against his own lamplight. Then, if he had a mind to, he could pepper the cabin with bullets. It wouldn't take long for one of them to find him. Cal knew that either way his chances weren't good.

As if in agreement, another bullet ripped into a box Cal was storing his canned supplies in. Peas and condensed milk burst open and the box exploded against the cabin wall.

'You goddamn, cowardly night trash,' he yelled, immediately troubled. For someone stupid enough to leave a light on, was he smart enough to figure a way out, he wondered.

'Yes,' Cal shouted. He grabbed his knife from beneath his cot, rolled across the floor to the back wall as the rifle cracked again in the night. The bullets were finding good and accurate range, but they were also giving Cal a fix on where they were coming from.

He was looking up at the hanging lamp when it exploded, the sound piercing his head. The hammered tin broke apart and oil spat across the cabin. In the deep blackness Cal didn't move. He watched fascinated as the wick flickered, as it caught the thin pool of oil that oozed under his cot.

Then he turned on to his back and drew his knees up under his chin. He lashed out, his feet forcing out three logs from the back wall.

'I hope you're runnin', feller,' he rasped.

But the rifleman wasn't, and calmly placed two more shots into the cabin. That was all right with Cal though. It meant that whoever it was, didn't know what Cal was up to; that he was out and making tracks for the ridge.

Fifty feet from his cabin, Cal crouched in a tangle of brush. He watched the flames reach out, hungrily lick around the frame of the window.

'That'll be the mattress . . . greasy buff'ler hide,' he muttered.

Then he ran, finding a path up the sharply sloping scree. He knew the trail and guessed, hoped it was the same one the rifleman had used. When he was within feet of the ridge, he stopped, turned back. The covering of his cabin was glowing yellow, swollen and taut from the heat below it.

'Cost me ten dollars, that roof,' he muttered, with increasing anger.

Then the tarp burst open and the fire lit the gulch. Burning fragments drifted into the night sky and Cal cursed for the loss of his meagre belongings. He made a lunge for the top of the ridge, rolled into the low mist that was already drifting through the scrubby pine.

Cal listened for the slightest sounds. He could only hear the fierce crackle from below as the logs of his cabin flared and split with the heat. Then he heard the yelling, the shouts from the miners as they made their way from the creek into the gulch. To his left, the rifleman fired again and Cal knew he was panicking, firing at his own demons, the dancing shadows.

Cal pushed his way fast but careful towards an outlying crop. The ground was hard, but carpeted in pine needles and it cushioned his approach. There was little noise from the fire now, only the rasp of his own eager breathing.

The ground mist along the ridge was waist-high; helped to muffle the grind and snap of a bullet being levered into the chamber of a rifle. But Cal caught the unmistakable sound and he went into a crouch, held dead still.

He heard the rifleman shifting his position, the hammer being pulled back. He half rose, moved forward, but the mist was confusing his sense of distance and he almost walked into the kneeling figure. The rifleman was on the outcrop, peering down at the low flames and smouldering cabin, the surrouding brush. The heat was spreading, brushing up the walls of the gulch, burning off the drifting mist as he pulled the trigger.

That was when the twig snapped under Cal's foot and the man swung round. He made a short, shocked sound and through the thin swirl of mist Cal saw the terrified face of Jeeter Krewel.

As the man levered another round and swung the rifle, Cal ducked and sprang. The shot reverberated around his head, but he hit the ground unharmed. With movement brought of despair and survival, he pushed himself up, swung the beaver knife in a great powerful arc.

The blade cut ruthlessly into Krewel's throat, and Cal pushed himself away.

The man was choking. He dropped his rifle and sagged into the ground. He tried to scream but emitted a repellent, bubbling howl.

Cal tossed the knife aside and got to his feet, grabbed down at the man's soaking, sticky collar.

'Why'd you come here?' he snarled angrily. 'You must know I ain't worth diddly squat.'

'It ain't that. Henner . . . must . . . told you 'bout . . . me,' the man slavered.

'Yeah. It was you an' him in Las Cruces,' Cal recalled.

The man's last words ended in a bloody gurgle.

'You . . . killed Waxy Bittleman. I couldn't . . . just . . . had to come . . . lookin'. You musta known my name . . . you'd o' come lookin' . . . . always.'

Cal touched the livid scar across his forehead.

'Yeah, you're right,' he told him. 'You'd never have laid easy in your bed. But that's all changed now, *Trooper*.' Cal loosed his fingers, dropped him to the ground to die.

Cal picked up the rifle, opened and closed the breech, backed off when he heard a shuffle somewhere in the brush. Then he heard Pug Edgcumbe's guarded voice.

'Crow? Cal?'

Cal looked down at the dead rifleman. The body lay shrouded in the wisps of remaining ground mist. Cal suddenly shivered, realized he was going to need a new coat.

'Keep comin', Pug,' he answered. 'There's nothin' here to give you trouble.'

In the darkness, Cal saw the dark figure of the miner walk on to the outcrop. He was carrying a heavy-gauge shotgun, stopped short when he saw the body of Krewel.

'Jesus. He was doin' the shootin'?' he asked, incredulous. 'They ain't wastin' any time, are they?'

Cal shook his head. 'This ain't anythin' to do with claim-jumpin', Pug. It's an ol' friend who wanted somewhere to die.'

Pug said nothing. He looked confused, bent to have a look at the dead man.

Cal turned his attention to the gulch floor as the flames from his cabin blazed up again.

'That'll be the can o' coal oil. There's some pitch in there as well,' he said quietly.

'I've never seen this bird before,' Pug told him. 'All shootin's are supposed to be reported to the agency, Cal.'

'Yeah, you told me that,' Cal replied, stepping over to retrieve his knife. 'I hope they ain't gonna give me any trouble, Pug,' he added sarcastically.

'Naagh, I'm the president, don't forget.'

Cal kneeled, drew his knife-blade through the damp earth a few times, then slowly straightened up. He looked down to where the blaze of his cabin was finally dying down.

'I hadn't forgot, Pug. An' them rats down there'll have to get 'emselves a new address before tomorrow night,' he added.

'You can start over. You will, if you're serious about stayin' . . . an' there's plenty o' timber,' Pug said earnestly.

Cal thought for a moment, poked a boot at Krewel's body.

'You goin' to report this?'

'Got to. An' maybe we'll lose the body on the way into town,' Pug offered.

Cal held on to the rifle, had his final word as he walked from the outcrop.

'Yeah. In the dark, I guess that could happen. He's more'n likely to fall from his horse.'

Nine hours later, the San Simon Agency met in Sego Bench In Jimes's Livery Stable, a small group of men gathered around Pug Edgcumbe. In an hour, at least twenty miners appeared before those few called in to adjudicate, and their squabbles and boundary problems were quickly dealt with before the chairman called for order. He rapped an axe-handle against a cleet barrel.

'Listen up. Let's have some order now,' Pug demanded of them, before carrying on. 'Most of you know by now, that a feller named Krewel was killed last night . . . early this mornin', while attemptin' to bush-whack Calvin Crow, out along the creek.'

'What we doin' here then Pug? You say he was a bush-whacker,' a man interrupted.

'We're here to say our good riddances in proper order. I take it you ain't protestin' at that, Cletus?'

'No I surely ain't, Pug. There's a number of us here who'd wish more murderin' scum would get spiked. We all got more names.'

Pug allowed Cletus a short chorus of approval, then nodded considerately, lifted the axe-handle.

'The Agency of San Simon hereby and duly clears Calvin Crow of any unlawful killin'.' Pug caught Cal's eye, glanced at the miners around him. 'That means you're all free to reconvene in the chairman's bar, if you've a mind.'

A few of the men stopped to shake Cal's hand, or pat him on the back. The others were already heading for the nearest saloon.

Pug beckoned to Cal, introduced him to four of the agency adjudicators.

'Cal, I'd like you to meet Nathan Bowler, Don Bonito, Harvey Elms an' Macey Hume.'

'I can add to some o' them names Cletus was talkin' about,' Harvey Elms said enthusiastically.

'That goes for all of us,' Pug muttered in agreement. 'Heard somethin' this mornin, Cal,' he then said. 'Nathan here's just got back from Las Cruces. Seems the state has named Denton Farwell Lome as sheriff o' the San Simon Territory.' Pug spoke without sway or inflection in his voice.

Cal tried the same. 'Now, *there*'s a man who knows how to impose law an' order,' he said.

'Yeah, send 'em on to Sego Bench. I've heard about Marshal Lome,' Elms said. 'Any o' you boys feel better knowin' that he's comin' to town?' he asked.

'No, not much,' Nathan Bowler offered. 'Last week a neighbour o' mine had his claim jumped by a pair o'

108

Frisco Gentle's dogs. I wonder if the new sheriff'll have anything to say about that?'

The speculation on Lome's appointment ended then, and Cal hitched a ride back to the creek in Pug's mule-wagon. In mid-afternoon he moved into the gulch, spent the rest of the day rebuilding, tying-in his last timbers. He made a three-sider, up tight to the side of the gulch. Then he hacked out some of the rock at the rear of his new cabin, built a cot space in the nook. He made a raft of poles for the roof, piled on mud and stones from the creek.

It was nearly full dark before he'd finished, and the finished structure gave Cal a lot more protection, both from the weather and from the possibility of a second attempt on his life from the ridge.

Pug had loaned him some dollars, and the following day Cal borrowed the mule wagon to take into Sego Bench. He purchased only essential supplies, and once again it was some time after mid-day by the time he returned to his claim.

For four hours he bent to his seam, only to find the oxides running thin. Darkness was fast running into the gulch when he thought he'd made a find around the base of a long flat boulder.

'I'm goin' to cut in,' he told Pug at their late meal. 'Make a run along the bed . . . blast out the rock if I have to. I'm sure there's some gain there.'

Pug nodded wisely as he sliced his Dark Mule.

'Whatever happens . . . just remember to put the light out,' he said, and smiled.

\*

The next morning, Cal worked from sun-up until noon. He split and levered out boulders, and filled his hand-cart with a likely mix of grit and mud slurry. After the creek wash, there was enough silver grain to pay back Pug and a whole lot more. Enough for a new blanket coat an' a bag full of eggs, he told himself.

Cal's hard work along the gulch bed had run him up to a stand of fallen dead nut pine. An hour before dusk he used the pick to lever up one of the half-rotten trunks. The old timber was sheltering a rich aggregate of crushed shale, and in the last of the day's good light he saw the trace of glittering blue grain. He heaved the decaying trunks to one side, the exhilaration of his find giving him more muscle. But eventually his legs gave way and he buckled, got close to the deposits of precious ore.

Working by lamplight, it was full dark before Cal had gleaned the vein. He didn't quit until the wonder of finding was blunted by fatigue, until the pail was nearly half-filled at his feet.

Based on what the old flattened peach can had held, he'd taken up more than a thousand dollars in six hours.

He felt he should be exultant, but he remembered Pug Edgcumbe's advice. He pushed the beaver-knife into a crevice above his head and pinched out the light. He listened intently for a moment before closing his eyes and thinking; thinking he'd buy that Frontier Colt from Ellwood's. Within two hours he was asleep, the fingertips of one hand buried in the blue stuff at his side.

# 13
# The Cut

Lauren Garth woke suddenly. The room was in darkness and for a while she wondered where she was. She lay still, then rubbed her eyes, brushed the hair from her face. The sounds of the street drifted through the partly open windows; the raised voices of men, their stamp along the boardwalk. She listened to the piercing squeal of a dry axle as a freighter rolled past on its way to the roaring camp, Lordsburg and Las Cruces. She raised her head, gave the driver some bar-room abuse.

She sat up and swung her legs from her bed, stared into the darkness. Then she reached out to a small table and lit a decorative lamp. The coloured shade warmed the room, and the rich furnishings were suddenly reassuring.

It was there on the newly renovated first floor of the Arizona Rose, that Lauren had heaped her attention; fancy trappings gathered from the pages of a mail-order catalogue.

The partnership with Franklin Henner had prospered. Now there were drapes at the windows and wool rugs covered the puncheon floor. She had a closet filled with day and evening dresses, slippers and wraps of French silk. They were the material rewards of what she'd achieved since arriving in Sego Bench; since her first weepy night in Lyle Roach's room at the Mariposa Hotel.

She looked lazily around the room, walked to the window alcove. She sat at her dressing-table and pushed coloured glass bottles to one side, sighed for not knowing what she wanted out of life, what she'd get.

There was a tentative rap on the door, and she turned to face it.

'Yes,' she called out, fairly certain she knew who it was.

'It's me, Frank, let me in,' Henner said in his normal manner.

Lauren grabbed a shawl and moved to the door. She stood to one side and let him step into the room.

'I got to talk to you, Lauren.' The concern was clear in Henner's voice.

'OK. Shut the door and sit down. It sounds like trouble,' she said.

'Yeah, it could be. I don't know yet.' Henner took a deep breath before he continued. 'We've done good here in Sego Bench, Lauren. We're gettin' rich. In a year . . . if the yield lasts that long . . . we'll both be able to retire.'

Lauren gave a thin smile. 'Nice thought, Frank. But that's not "trouble", an' it's not what you came here to tell me.'

Henner rubbed his hands together nervously.

'No it's just that . . . well, you know the high-graders, Lauren,' he said. 'The dirt crust that sits on top of a place like this. You know 'em as well as I do.'

'Maybe. What are you sayin', Frank?'

'They've had a meet ... got 'emselves organized. Denton Lome's headin' 'em up.'

'Yeah, I'd heard that too. But we're not miners, Frank.'

'No, we ain't miners, Lauren, but it affects us. All the silver that's shipped out's goin' back to Las Cruces. Only from now on, it ain't gonna get there. I doubt if a single grain will ever make it to a bank. The miners have got the only force to go up against Lome ... them an' their agency. But I can't see 'em wantin' to take on a serious fight.' Henner looked up gravely. 'I've been told we've got to choose ourselves a brand. *That's* what I'm sayin', Lauren.'

'What're you goin' to do? What are *we* goin' to do?'

'We ain't up to fightin' them either. That means handin' over a percentage of our turnover.'

'They take a cut? How much?' Lauren demanded.

'They ain't worked out the figure yet. Whatever it is, it'll be enough to leave us alone. Maybe all *our* stuff'll get to Las Cruces.'

Lauren bridled, her face tight and angered.

'We're payin' for "maybe"?'

'Yeah. They'll put in their own cappers ... keep an eye on the take.'

'What other names you got ... other than Lome?' Lauren asked.

'None for certain. But *he's* plenty, you know that. He's mean an' he's tough, Lauren. He'll put Sego Bench into his shadow. You forgot Las Cruces already?'

'Hell, Frank, I thought I handled the melodramatics. What you're sayin' is, your belly's flappin'. What happens if we don't pay?'

'He'll kill us. Get himself the biggest cut of all. He can't lose.'

Lauren shrugged, suddenly felt the early morning chill. She moved towards the window and held back the curtain, looked down into the darkness of the street.

'We've both got a lot to lose, Frank . . . everything,' she said. 'You're goin' to have to do more than wheedle or whinge. You've got money . . . use it.'

'Yeah, I will, Lauren. I just needed you to tell me. I reckon there is a way,' he added enigmatically.

Henner got to his feet and crossed the room. He opened and closed Lauren's door quietly, stood for a few moments in the hallway, thinking.

Lauren continued to watch the shadowy street movements from her window.

'No goddamn marshal from Las Cruces is goin' to bulldog me,' she said chillingly.

It was almost two in the morning, but when Henner went back down to the main room of the Arizona Rose, there were men still drinking and gambling.

Denton Lome sat alone at a table by the wall furthest from the street. Henner dragged a chair across to him and sat down.

'You come to jaw or play cards?' Lome asked without looking up.

'Jaw. A lot o' men who come into this place like to do just that, Marshal,' Henner said. 'Just recently, one of 'em was tellin' me somethin' interestin'. Said that in El Paso there's been rewards posted for Border Troopers. Most of 'em from Barkdale. A thousand dollars for each man. How about that?'

114

'Interestin'. Got any names?'

'Yeah. From what I recall, Dillard Groff, Jeeter Krewel an' Crick Gibson were three of 'em.' Henner got more involved in his task, pulled the chair in close to the table.

'I can tell you what happened to Dillard Groff, an' it weren't nice.' Henner pressed the issue. 'Krewel . . . well you must o' heard about him. But the other one . . . yeah, he *does* sound interestin'. He turned up in Las Cruces. Him an' Krewel were on their way to Mexico apparently. Only that's when the trail runs cold, Marshal. Seems this Crick Gibson just disappeared . . . like he never existed.'

Lome looked at Henner, his customary self-importance waning.

'Like Groff,' he said.

'No, not like Groff. I just told you. Calvin Crow stuck a Green River knife into *him*. From the front, but it must o' severed his spine. Sound like the work of someone familiar, Marshal?'

Lome's face became more expressive, drawn with concern. He repeated Calvin Crow's name, slowly.

'How'd you know all this, Henner?' he then asked.

'Don't matter. But I tell you this Marshal, if *I*'d ever been anywhere near that camp at Barkdale, *I*'d be worried . . . worried enough to stop me legs workin'. Calvin Crow's dangerous. He don't frighten an' he don't read the rules.'

Lome was going to spit into the floor, but his mouth was too dry. Without another word he got to his feet. He grinned sickly and carefully put one foot in front of the other, made for the street.

'Remember it was *you* put him on the coach, Marshal,'

Henner called out. His whole body was trembling. His face was wet with sweat, and he swabbed it with a large bandanna.


A full hour after Denton Lome had left the Arizona Rose, Jared Munroe hunkered uncomfortably in a rock-strewn draw. He was beyond the roaring camp, fifty yards off the wagon- and coach-road that led from Sego Bench to Lordsburg. It was approaching first light, and it seemed he'd been waiting for hours.

He took off his Stetson and clawed his fingers through his hair. Then he grabbed the barrel of Frisco Gentle's Winchester and, keeping low, made his way to the lip of the draw. He looked west, to where the road bent sharply through the broom and prickly pear. Then he swung his gaze east and saw the billowing veil of alkali dust, the creaking freighter on its way from Sego Bench.

For the second time that day, the old wagon and its driver got a mouthful of abuse as Munroe swore savagely. The freighter would have to pull over to let the stage overtake. 'But why there'? Munroe thought. 'Why now'? If he let the stage go because of that, Denton Lome would take his head off.

But it was too late to worry. He could see the stage approaching a quarter-mile distant. The fat driver, Chubby Pound, was driving fast and he too saw the freighter ahead of him. He started yelling for the wagon to move over and Munroe watched with bated breath.

He realized that if the wagon didn't clear the road completely, the coach would have to slow. He smiled grimly. Maybe he wouldn't have to wait for the coach to take the bend.

Munroe made up his mind, estimated he'd have the time. He rolled out of the draw, and went down the slope in a crouching run. When he got close to the road he steadied himself and levelled the Winchester. As the coach swung around the freighter back on to the road, he put a bullet close over Chubby's head.

The stage slewed as Chubby dropped his whip to pull on the brake. He looked up, saw Munroe ahead of him as he pulled the team to a halt.

One of the passengers elbowed himself into the open window and started yelling. He pushed a gun out and fired a panic-stricken shot across the desert. Munroe calmly put a bullet into the side panel of the coach and the man fell back inside with a bullet deep in his upper arm.

'Get out o' that box . . . all o' you,' Munroe yelled.

The coach door was flung open and two men climbed out. Their faces were pale and sullen and they looked back along the road, nervously.

'I want any dirt you're carryin'. Drop it in the road,' Munroe shouted at them. 'You, Chubby . . . throw the box down.'

Chubby Pound, shocked at recognizing Munroe, pulled the sturdy iron-strapped box from under his seat and dropped it to the ground.

Munroe swung the rifle at the two men, up at the wounded man still in the coach. Then he too looked back along the road, saw the freighter had turned and was heading back towards Sego Bench. He decided not to drop the old driver.

'Get that coach out o' here, Chubby. On to Lordsburg,' he shouted, then waited while the men climbed back aboard. He cracked the rifle-barrel hard against the side of the coach, and Chubby yelled for the team to move off.

He lifted the pokes from out of the dust, then dragged the ore-box off the road. Beside a thicket of chaparral he eased back the hammer of the Winchester.

It took two bullets to blow apart the lock on the strongbox, and inside were ten full leather pouches. They were all stamp-tagged with the owner's name and the amount, and Munroe aggregated them at exactly $2,000.

He allowed himself a satisfied smirk, then carried the box back through the draw to where he'd left his buckboard. He transferred the pokes to a saddle pouch on the driving-seat and climbed aboard.

He looked east, in the direction the coach was headed, considered going south, cross-country into Sonora. With that sort of money he could make it, get beyond the fear of being caught. But there was the prospect of more easy money. It was there for the taking, and he was greedy.

Grinning at his fortune, he swung the buckboard back to the road, headed west, back to Sego Bench.

The one-time cattle-rustler had just passed the last of the roaring camp tents when he saw the two riders ahead. The bearded horsemen were mounted on grey mares, took centre of the road. Munroe recognized them as miners' agency men who were regulating traffic in and out of town. When both men drew their rifles, Munroe knew he was in trouble.

118

'Let Denton Lome protect me. Just get away,' he thought fast, as he swung the buckboard frantically into the brush.

Nathan Bowler fired, and Munroe's horse shuddered in its traces. The stricken animal went down snorting, its body twisting wildly between the shafts. The buckboard heaved, folded instantly into the desert and Munroe was thrown forward.

He saw the bright cloudless sky, then semi-darkness as the sand pressed into his face. He drew his knees up and rolled over, his hands flat on the ground. He spat against a mouthful of dry grit and opened his eyes.

He grabbed his hat and got unsteadily to his feet. The side of his face and his shoulder were painful where he'd fallen against the shafts, but he'd broken no bones. When the two men rode up, he glanced at the over-turned buckboard, his eyes noting the Winchester and his saddle pouch.

'Real sorry about the horse,' Harvey Elms said. 'Nathan's more accustomed to swingin' a pick. If you handn't o' been in such an all fired hurry, he might just o' taken your arm off.'

Bowler waved his rifle. 'Get that Winchester,' he ordered.

Munroe picked his gun out of the sand. He sensibly swung it away, watched it land near the feet of Elms's horse.

'Now the saddle pouch,' Bowler said.

Munroe kneeled, had to drag the pouch from beneath the dead horse's rump.

Harvey Elms spat a thin stream of dark juice towards Munroe, wiped the back of his hand across his mouth.

'Cheer up, mister, we ain't gonna shoot you,' he rasped. 'The Miners' Agency's got to meet in Sego Bench . . . specially convened. Then they'll hang you at noon.'

# 14
# The Summons

The following weeks passed for Calvin Crow in a relentless haze of work. The need for vengeance was dulled, and when he thought of his son, Walker, he didn't any more think to search out the last of the men responsible for his death. It was still there though, but sleeping, deeper.

He was enjoying his strike, making himself curiously comfortable. Behind his cot space in the nook, he'd dug a hole, made a cache of half his silver ore. Along the bed of the gulch, under a rock that was home to a gila monster, he kept the other half. He had no immediate desire for the stash and almost felt concern for the man who went in search of it. For himself, day to day, and minding Pug Edgcumbe's caution, he kept a poke inside his shirt.

Movement along the creek continued relentless. Downstream water was fouled with the workings and rubbish of incoming miners, the waste from their mules. Cal had joined with Pug and two other miners to run a flume along the wall of the arroyo. He'd already built his own chute from there into his own claim where he tipped in his mud and grit slurry. With a constant water flood, he did twice the work in half the time.

The days got shorter, and long after first light the ground was rimed white, and ice crusted in the pots and pans. As the temperature dropped along the creek, resolute miners began their winter measures, but some of them left for the security and warmth of town work.

When the winds grew colder, Cal heaped his tailings against the walls of his cabin, bought himself a beaver coat and hat with flaps. One night he was sitting talking with Pug. They both wore their entire stock of clothing, toasted meat chunks in front of a fire. For Pug, the circumstances led him to state the obvious.

'You never came to Sego Bench to dig for silver, Cal. I know that,' he said. 'You might be cut out for this lonesome life, but I ain't. There's too much I miss.' Pug had a close look at his piece of rabbit. 'Heard a song once, about folk needin' other folk. I reckon they're right. For me anyway.'

'You've made your pile, an' you'll be goin' home soon, Pug,' Cal replied.

Pug nodded, spat some Dark Mule. 'Yeah, an' I won't be comin' back.' He looked across at Cal, and his expression changed. 'There's somethin' that's been worryin' me, Cal,' he started seriously. 'Gabe Hooker tried to get his grain out last week . . . gave it to a friend of his . . . name o' Wellington. He was goin' up in the hills for lumber. They found his body near Benson, full o' bullet holes. Dewey Larkin's claim's been jumped, an' he took a beatin'. I got a bad feelin' about all this, Cal. Who's goin' to be next?'

'You think it's goin' to be you?' Cal asked considerately.

'Yeah. I must be in line. That's why I want you to get the bags to Essie . . . if an' when.'

Pug pulled a piece of paper from deep within the folds of his clothes.

'I've written down the address. It's near Wichita. I told you that, didn't I?' he said uncomfortably. 'You know where I've made the stash,' he went on slowly. 'I reckon that's all that really matters.'

Cal took the piece of paper, shook his head. 'I'm guessin' your Essie thinks different,' he said. 'But I'll see she gets whatever you want. It'd be the least I could do . . . in the unlikely event.'

The two men quietly chewed their smoky meat. They looked up when they heard the approaching crunch of gulch shingle and Cal reached for his new Colt. A man leading a horse was moonlit in an area Cal had cleared out in front of his cabin.

'I'm lookin' for Pug Edgcumbe,' the man called out.

'What you want with him?' Cal came back.

'There's more trouble. We need him for a Miners' Agency meetin' in the mornin'. Harve Elms an' Nate caught the turkey who held up the Las Cruces stage. We're gonna stretch his neck.'

Cal groaned, eased down the hammer of his Colt.

'He wouldn't want to miss that. I'll see he gets there,' he called out.

'I knew it. It's the start of real trouble, Cal, an' I want you with me,' Pug said quietly, after the man had gone. 'We've got to find men . . . those who won't back down . . . put an end to this.'

# 15
# A Trial

The trail along San Simon Creek was bustling with miners. Of Jared Munroe and his capture, they spoke their minds, loudly and defiantly. But they were together, and there was no one facing them down, Cal thought to himself as he and Pug made their way into town.

Traffic had come to a standstill, and now people jammed the streets of Sego Bench. Someone shouted when they saw Pug, and he raised an acknowledging hand.

'Where's Munroe?' he asked.

'Over here, Pug,' a voice shouted back.

Cal looked across the street, saw the one-time cattle thief with his hands tied to a hitching rail. There was some bruising across his face and he wore a hapless grin.

'Got any last words?' the miner called Cletus yelled at him.

Cal heard Munroe's hopeful reply.

'I ain't dead yet, muckman.'

'Howdy, Ninian,' Pug said, and shook hands with a short, sharply dressed man. He introduced Cal. 'Cal, this

124

is Ninian Ellwood. He owns the variety store an' he's on the town committee.'

'We've done business,' Cal said, and shook the man's small hand.

Ellwood looked at Pug. 'Hammond Gow's an attorney and he's agreed to handle the legal stuff,' he said seriously.

'We don't want anythin' legal to get in the way of what we got to do. He was caught red-handed, so he'll get what he deserves. Let's start the proceedings.' Pug grated.

Hammond Gow wore a tight suit and looked pale and ill; he had beads of greasy sweat across his top lip. The man was in control, and although his hands were damp and trembling, his voice sounded strong and confident.

'We got to do this accordin' to state law . . . at least be seen to be doin' it,' he said loudly.

The attorney, who was on his way to Tucson and Phoenix, was instantly hooted at.

'You know none o' that legislation's got here yet. In Sego, we got our own agency laws,' Cletus shouted out. 'Let's just telegraph him home.'

When others immediately joined in the outcry for Munroe's neck, Cal looked uncertainly around him. For a while, groups of angry men shuffled about, then reluctantly moved aside when a horseman pushed his way through them.

The man was Oaky Bunns, and he flaunted a silver star on the lapel of his black coat.

'Sounds like you hillbillies are about to break the law,' he rumbled from his big, heavily bearded face.

Ninian Ellwood was standing between Pug and Cal.

125

'Sheriff Lome's appointed Bunns his deputy. Now we got that scum ridin' our streets with impunity,' he said.

'Yeah, I've met their sort before,' Cal told him.

'You best get outa here Oaky,' a man shouted. 'We got ourselves a long piece o' hemp.'

Cal looked up at Bunns, saw his eyes searching for the man who'd spoken. Then Bunns saw Cal, and his face darkened. He kicked his spurs and the horse lunged forward. It was a Bunns ploy, and Cal grinned as he leaped to one side.

'He'll do that once too often,' he said, to no one in particular.

'Yeah, I heard about the first time,' Ellwood bit out as Bunns rode off.

A lumber wagon was rolled up in front of the Long Lizard saloon and Munroe was pushed up aboard. Hammond Gow climbed up beside him, and Pug and Ellwood followed.

Cal moved into the pressing, growling, crowd. He nodded to a few men he knew, heard a few more speak his name. The fight he'd had with Oaky Bunns and the killing of Krewel had made him another man to be feared.

For the sake of all those nearby, Gow started on the gist of his case. After two minutes, from among the people that thronged the street at least half raucously offered their services as jurors. Cal made his way back to the wagon as Nathan Bowler and Harvey Elms were being introduced as witnesses.

'Reckon you all know what we're here for,' Gow shouted out. Cal noticed the attorney's appearance had improved a little.

'This man is typical of the lawlessness . . . the free-for-all that has become San Simon,' he started. 'A lot of you have been robbed . . . brutally beaten . . . lost your claims. For the past few weeks there's been no one who's got their stash much further than the roaring camp. Now there's as much silver bein' buried in the ground as what's been taken from it. You ain't even safe with pennies in your pocket along this street any more.'

Gow saw the miners were getting more keyed up. He held out his hands, continued to incite.

'Despite the state appointin' Denton Lome as sheriff of this territory, there's no law but what you've made yourselves, and, dare I say . . . enforced. It's by *those* rules, that you've made thieving from any mine or miner in the San Simon a capital offence . . . a hanging offence.'

A pistol shot rang out in the street and a shout went up.

'Let the harpy swing. We've wasted enough time out here.'

'He ain't killed nobody,' somebody contributed half-heartedly, as the jurymen entered the saloon.

'An' he ain't said who he's workin' with, either,' Cal added, almost in approval.

For the ten minutes the group considered their verdict, the miners in the street got more restless.

Pug leaned over the side of the wagon.

'Thank God they've finished. They're comin' out now.'

The jury, which Cal recognized as the agency commit-tee, stomped down the shallow steps of the saloon. They had a foreman, and he had a word with Gow, handed him up a slip of paper.

'What's it say?' Cletus demanded.

'To the letter? "Guilty. Give him the ice water",' Gow told him.

'What's that mean?' a gruff voice behind Cal wanted to know.

'It's *hot* where Munroe's goin',' he told him.

There was a low, menacing rumble and the crowd pushed forward. Pug held up his hands and yelled at them.

'You ain't havin' him. We'll carry on doin' it proper.'

The men stopped, agitatedly listened to what else Pug had to say.

'The foreman says it was unanimous. Take it easy, there's no argument.'

Cal shook his head at the conflict. He knew there were some folk who wanted a change for the better: social order in Sego Bench. But watching Jared Munroe choke on the end of a rope wasn't going to get them there.

Cletus was still provoking the miners and they began to push forward again.

'We ain't arguin'. We're gettin' on with the doin',' he threatened.

There was no doubting the feeling of the men. Pug grimaced as he swung down from the wagon.

'I ain't goin' up against them boys . . . not for the likes o' Munroe,' he said to Cal, his voice drowned out by what had suddenly become an incensed mob.

Cletus, and the man with the length of new rope, climbed up the tailgate of the wagon. There was already a well-formed hangman's knot, and Cletus tossed the other end up and over an overhang of the saloon.

Cal saw Munroe's wretched grin had disappeared. The guilty man's muscles were tense and his eyes flitted nervously, as the man with the noose end took a step along the wagon bed towards him. Cletus muttered under his breath, tossed the other end down to two men who were standing close by.

Then there was another movement from along the street and the crowd turned. From thirty, forty yards away, Cal saw Denton Lome riding straight towards them.

Cal was dumbfounded, remembered someone once telling him that life and death was all about good and bad timing.

With a revengeful grin, Oaky Bunns rode stirrup to stirrup with Lome. Two others rode close behind. They led a spare mount, made a show of their sawed-off shotguns.

The miners hushed their noise as the four horsemen clattered up to the lumber wagon. The man who'd built the noose was just about to place it around Munroe's neck, but he didn't, he stopped moving. Like most of the others, he was fearful of the newly appointed sheriff. Munroe's face was deathly pale, but a thin smile of relief appeared.

'What in the name of Hades is goin' on here?' Lome rasped at the men who started to back away from him. 'Looks like an ol' fashioned necktie party.' The sheriff studied the wary, worried faces. 'Well, I'll just have to break it up. I don't want you "vigilantes" doin' something you'll regret . . . and believe me, you will. I don't know if Munroe's guilty or not, but he'll get a fairer trial in Las Cruces.'

'Yeah, an' I'm Geronimo.' Cletus jumped off to the ground. He walked up to Lome's big claybank horse, his face puffy and indignant. 'That thief'll never get to Las Cruces . . . you'll make sure o' that, Lome. He's one o' your dog-pack.'

Lome swung his horse's flank, at the same time moved his right hand, fast. The barrel of his short-tooled carbine slashed down, and Cletus fell to the warm, raised dirt of the street.

Cal winced at the dull crack of steel on bone. He pulled the brim of his Stetson down across the front of his face. The odds weren't good and it wasn't the place to go up against Lome.

The carbine turned on the crowd, and the miners backed away.

'I'm the law here,' Lome stated flatly. His voice carried in the abrupt silence that fell. 'You will remember that.'

Cletus moved his legs, put a hand to his head. His face was split and the blood ran freely through his fingers, down the arm of his heavy workshirt. Lome glanced down at him, his face expressionless.

'Oaky, get the boys to take him out to the poles. Ten days for threatening behaviour, an' another ten 'cause it was me.'

There was a menacing buzz from the disgruntled miners, and Cal looked across at Pug. As president of their agency, the men expected him to say something, to challenge, dispute Denton Lome's office. They had the numbers, if not the guns, to badger the sheriff. But the man's reputation rode before him, and it curbed all their nerves.

Lome threw a hostile look around him, snapped his carbine back into its sheath.

'You people get back to your work. Clear the street, now!' he shouted at them. Then he looked up at the wagon, spoke to the man still standing close to Munroe. 'You. I ever see you with more than a shovel in your hands, I'll shoot you dead. Now turn the prisoner loose.'

With a severe look at the would-be hangman, Munroe held out his hands to be freed. Then he climbed from the wagon, snatched up the reins of the spare horse.

Cal knew Pug was watching him. The miner told him he'd wanted his help. But for Cal that wasn't enough and he couldn't condone a lynching. And then the opportunity was gone. Riding with Bunns, Munroe was almost jeering as they reined in at the east end of town.

The miners had taken heed of Lome's order to clear the street. In less than five minutes, they'd dispersed and the town sounded and looked unusually deserted.

Lome didn't recognize Cal. He walked his horse to the middle of the street, looked up at the windows of the two-storey buildings. Then he rode slow and steady to meet with Bunns and Munroe, cantered off to where the north slope angled up the canyon.

Pug pulled down and looped up the hanging rope. He glanced at Cal as he tossed it into the back of the wagon.

'Guess we won't be needin' this, after all,' he said resentfully. 'Funny how your guts run, when you're ten feet from the workin' end of a carbine.'

'It weren't much to do with guts, Pug. The whole affair was doubtful . . . an' you know it. You did the right thing by stayin' alive,' Cal said quietly.

Pug turned his attention to the saloon's entrance.

'Maybe, but I'll never know if there was anyone to follow if I led,' he responded stoically. 'I'm goin' in there . . . gettin' bug juiced 'til I see the long lizard.'

# 16
# No More Trouble

When the riders got to Hamey Barge's cabin, Jared Munroe almost fell to the ground. It was after they'd cleared town that the shock first got to him, and now his hands shook and his legs nearly buckled under him.

'You looked scared back there, Munroe. Thought we'd have to scrape you up,' Bunns taunted.

Munroe took a few deep breaths, looked up.

'Yeah, I was. Scared to death,' he said dully. 'Now you know, you can shut your ugly great mouth. You understand, cow head?'

Frisco Gentle was standing on the low step of the cabin to meet them.

'Oaky don't mean nothin',' he said, 'he's too stupid.'

Denton Lome rode his big claybank up close, held up his hand. The metal of his new sheriff's star glinted bright in the afternoon sun.

'I told you I wouldn't let you swing. You remember, Jared?'

'Yeah, I remember. But you never mentioned how close you'd run it.'

Lome smirked. 'I never saw that knife man . . . Calvin Crow, around,' he said.

'He was there, Denton, I saw him. He probably scampered off when he saw you comin',' Bunns sneered.

The men moved into the cabin and Hamey Barge produced two bottles of whiskey and some glasses. Munroe rattled in a brimful and downed it in one pull. He banged the empty glass on the table, looked at the tremble of his hands.

'What's next, Sheriff?' he asked half-heartedly.

'Nothin' for you, cowboy,' Lome replied. 'It'll take a week for you to stop shakin'. You stay here . . . play some poker with Hamey. Get him to pour the drinks.'

The others sniggered, and Munroe smiled thinly.

'What happens then?' he persisted.

'Nothin',' Lome snapped back. 'Nothin' as far as you're concerned. If anyone comes sniffin' around, Hamey can tell 'em I'm waitin' for a charge-sheet to arrive from Las Cruces. In the meantime, I'll be plannin' somethin' else. Them miners are goin' to be squeezed.'

'Sego Bench ain't goin' to forget today,' Munroe said, taking the second bottle of whiskey from Barge. 'But what happens next time? Them miners' were that close to getting sparked.'

'Yeah, that's right, Denton,' Bunns said. 'We got that loudmouth Cletus Brand, but Pug Edgcumbe's the one they listen to. He's the president o' that goddamned agency an' he's dangerous.'

'Yeah, maybe you're right,' Lome said, looking closely at Munroe. 'Perhaps I'm wrong about keepin' you cooped up, Jared. Now you've earned your spurs, perhaps it's only right that you take care of the old fool.

It wasn't more'n a few hours ago that he was ready to clap to your toes dancin in the dust.'

Suddenly the frailty in Munroe's legs seemed worse. Caught between volatile, outraged miners and Denton Lome was a real bad place to be. But he nodded slowly.

'What do you want me to do?' he asked with foreboding.

Lome stopped in the doorway, turned around as he was leaving. His pale eyes fastened on Munroe.

'Make sure Edgcumbe ain't fit to lead them miners. I don't want him causin' me any more trouble,' he said menacingly, then walked out to his horse.

# 17
# An Added Touch

Calvin Crow had finished off his peas and cheese pie, was draining the last of his coffee when Clooney Piper came up to him.

'You're Calvin Crow?' he asked tentatively.

Cal had never seen Piper before, but he recognized a man who spent his time at a card-table.

'Yeah. What can I do for you?'

The gambler shook his head.

'Nothin' for me. It's Lauren Garth, wants to see you.' Piper shrugged and left the restaurant.

Cal put his empty coffee cup down, for a few seconds built a mind picture of Lauren Garth. Three dollars was the inflated price of the meal and he placed the money beside his cleared plate.

After the ruckus with Jared Munroe and Denton Lome, the town remained quiet. There were few men on the street; as though they'd been badly scared.

The day had turned to night, and a touch of cold blew

in from the distant Nama Altos. He buttoned his new plaid coat, looked towards the Arizona Rose.

He tried to work out what Lauren could possibly want with him. He hadn't seen her for weeks. He didn't understand why, but on occasion, when he'd been in town late, he'd avoided the saloon when she'd been singing.

The unusual calm that was holding the rest of the town didn't extend itself to the Arizona Rose. Along the front of the building, tar torches flared yellow in the crisp air. Inside, the miners were hard at it, drinking and gambling, unreceptive to the tuneless jangle of the pianola. Cal had a beer and a whiskey chaser, thought it was a little early for Lauren to be making her appearance. He caught the attention of the barman who'd served him.

'Where's Miss Garth?' he asked.

'Right above us,' the man answered directly and turned away.

Cal nodded, wondered on the whereabouts of Frank Henner, but didn't ask. He pushed his way to the end of the room; men were crowding the bar one side, sitting at busy tables the other.

There was an open door at the end of the bar with a hard-looking man propped in the doorway. He looked hostilely at Cal, pushed out an arm to bar his entry.

'Miss Lauren's expectin' me,' Cal said, respecting the fact that the man had a job to do.

The man nodded. 'Crow, yeah. Go on up.'

Cal brushed past the guard and went towards the staircase. On the first floor he walked down the shadowy hall to where the barman said Lauren's room would be.

From a half-open door, lamplight fell across an ornate carpet-runner. He rapped on the doorframe. There was a rustle, movement in the room and Lauren stepped forward. For her nightly appearance she was sheathed in a blue satin evening gown. The light glistened on her chestnut coloured hair, and her pale face met his openly. She smiled, friendly-looking.

'I didn't think you'd come.'

'Don't tell me. It's because you're a woman like you.'

Lauren gave a small laugh.

'No, Cal. It's because I couldn't see you changin' the habits of the past few weeks.'

Disarmed a little at the riposte, Cal followed her into the room. He looked around, whistled at the plush furnishings. Not since his wedding-night in San Antonio, Texas, had he felt so immediately beguiled, and the memory nipped at his vitals.

Lauren tugged a lock of her hair.

'I told you once, I liked the way you worried Denton Lome,' she said without explanation.

'Yeah, I remember. We were on the coach.'

'You remember everythin' I say?'

'To me, yeah . . . both sentences.'

For the second time since they'd first met, Lauren wondered if Calvin Crow did have any feelings.

'You look different,' she tried.

'So do you. Is this what you wanted to see me for? See what I looked like?'

She stood close to him.

'No, it wasn't *exactly* that,' she said.

He coughed and took off his hat, leaned in close. He kissed her softly for a few seconds. He drew back a frac-

tion, then pushed his face in again, firmer and a tad
longer. Then he pulled away and smiled, gave another
little cough.

'Was it *that*, then? I knew it would be good,' he said.

'So did I,' she answered appealingly, but serious. 'But
no, it's not that Cal. It's your friend, Pug Edgcumbe.'

'Pug? Where is he? What's happened to him?'

'After you left him at the Long Lizard, he came here.
He's been drinkin' hard ever since . . . said he'd let the
miners down . . . should've stood up to Lome.'

Lauren stared sadly at Cal, who was waiting to hear
more.

'But they let *him* down. They think a bit like you, and
that's how it'll end. You'll probably all die toughin' it out
on your own.'

As she crossed to a door opposite the windows, Cal
saw a watery gleam in the corner of her eye.

'I'm not sayin' any more. He's in here . . . just take
him,' she said, but not unkindly.

She opened the door, and through the gap Cal saw
Pug sprawled across a bed.

Lauren watched impassively as Cal pulled Pug from
the bed, folded him over his shoulder. As he turned
through the door, he thought to ask Lauren:

'You mentioned Denton Lome earlier. What's he got
to do with this?'

'You were there, weren't you? Pug said that Lome was
behind it all.'

Cal didn't answer. He went out and the door closed
quietly behind him. At that moment it would have been
so easy to leave Pug propped against the banisters for a
while and go back. But he readjusted the weight and

went on, stepped heavily down the hall to the stairs.

In the saloon bar, the customers watched Cal as he went through. They moved aside, but none spoke and none followed him. Outside he looked up and down the street. Pug was hefty, but he saw the man's old mud-wagon. It was still outside the livery stable, the mule patiently standing with its nose deep in an oat-bag.

When he rolled him into the rear of the wagon, Pug stirred, tried to raise himself.

'You've had a rough day, friend, an' you ain't goin' anywhere except home,' Cal said.

Like the town, the canyon along San Simon Creek was quiet. It was cold too, with early frost forming on the tips of the cheatgrass. Across the slope one or two lights shone through canvas walls, and up towards the ridge a coyote barked.

Cal got Pug through the door of his cabin, almost made it to the makeshift cot.

From the hard floor, Pug dragged himself upright and staggered, stared around him.

'Hey,' he yelled, making a startled grab in the darkness.

'Oh no you don't, old feller. I've had enough sex for one day,' Cal said, shaking his head and turning for the door.

The hard work of getting Pug from the wagon had made Cal sweat, and the sharp chill air hit him. He shivered, walked fast to the annexed gulch.

Inside his hole-up cabin he lit two happy-jack lamps. He picked up his beaver knife, hurled it with force against the logged wall. Then he poured a good measure of corn and climbed into his warm niche.

'Just let 'em try,' he muttered, and sighted his new, shiny Colt. He left the lamps burning, lay awake until first light.

# 18
# Snakebite

It was still early morning when Pug croaked a greeting at Cal. He was soaked to the skin, from where he'd lain full length in the icy water of the creek. He stood shaking with the cold, and he had a throbbing head, but he was sober.

'If that was you got me back last night, then I'm grateful to you, friend,' he said.

'We're all entitled to a drink now and then Pug. And better to die of that than pneumonia. Get back an' warm yourself. I'll see you later,' Cal shouted back.

Cal watched him go, then returned to work his claim. Miners were now leaving the San Simon at a steady rate; but curiously, it was the failed ones. Cal wanted to tell them they'd be safe enough if they had nothing worth stealing. Even a desperate outlaw would know that.

The sky was grey and cloudless, snow was heading from the north. The cold was getting worse, ate into Cal's bones if he didn't keep moving. Still, it was an ill wind, and he was lucky enough to get hold of another buffalo hide and a small belly-stove from a scared-off miner.

142

In the days that followed Jared Munroe's escape from a summary hanging, there were occasional meetings of the Miners' Agency in Sego Bench. But Cal wasn't a meetings man, and stayed away. Pug didn't refer back to the incident or his rendezvous with the bottle, and Cal didn't mention it either. But one evening when Cal was chopping firewood, he called by.

'I'm leavin', Cal. I've told 'em in town. I had to tell the agency. I won't be here in the mornin',' was what he had to say.

'That's soon, but it ain't much of a surprise, Pug. If you'd told me earlier, I could o' cut you that Christmas pine.'

Pug smiled solemnly.

'I'm goin' after midnight. I'll beat the law that way . . . if you know what I mean. I've sold the wagon . . . didn't think it was any use to you. I've got me a one-way mare. I won't be goin' east or west though, oh no. In Kansas we call it the black road. I'll be goin' into New Mexico. Ridin' easy, it shouldn't take more'n a week to get to Albuquerque. Get me the train back to Wichita.'

'Then I'll be wishin' you well, old friend. But seems like I owe you somethin' . . . the claim's makin' good,' Cal said.

Pug dribbled, half spat some Dark Mule juice into the ground.

'If you want to pay me back, come visit Great Bend. Let me see you're still alive.'

Pug didn't make much more of his leaving, and Cal appreciated it. The miner only had one more thing to say as he walked off.

'Get yourself a woman. It ain't too difficult. That

143

pretty singer at the Arizona Rose ... Lauren Garth ... she'll do.'

When Pug had gone, Cal built and lit a stove fire. He was used to, didn't mind isolation, but suddenly he felt loneliness. He probably wouldn't have done if Pug hadn't mentioned Lauren Garth.

It was in the first hours of the morning when Cal heard the gunshot. He guessed he'd been asleep, was flustered when he rolled to the floor. In the flat silence that immediately followed, he could hear the wind soughing over his cabin. He stomped into his boots and pulled on his coat, pushed his Colt into a side-pocket.

It was starry dark and the snow was real close. Cal swore at the cold, tried to place the sound. But he knew it could only come from one place and he started running. He saw the lights as soon as he broke through the scrub at the entrance to the gulch.

Three men were carrying lanterns. They were standing outside Pug Edgcumbe's cabin, moved aside as Cal ran forward. When he cleared the door, they closed in behind him, held up their lamps. Under the yellowish light, Cal saw the measure of the gunshot.

Pug lay in a dark pool of blood, on his back with his head twisted sideways. His eyes were open and his lips were drawn back in a grisly scowl. His left arm was stretched out, his fingers grasping the edge of the hollow he'd scooped to hide his full pokes.

Cal kneeled and eased Pug's other arm from underneath him. He looked at Pug's contorted face, at the black puncture holes on the heel of his bloodied hand.

'Jesus,' he rasped, 'they brought a diamond-back with

'em. Must o' tortured him . . . then let it bite him. The bullet in his back was just to make sure he died.'

'I saw 'em Cal,' Harvey Elms said. 'I was comin' to see Pug . . . see if he was really goin' to leave. I saw all of 'em ride off.'

'All of 'em? You saw all of 'em?' Cal glared at Elms.

'Yeah. It was Bunns an' Frisco Gentle. Munroe was with 'em.'

Cal walked up close to the man, who lowered his lantern.

'You sure? For their sake be *real sure*, mister,' he demanded, his voice spiked with menace.

'I'm sure. Me an' Nate should've put a bullet through Munroe's head when we caught him. Pug could've tugged his rope, hung him in the street.'

Cal took Elms's lantern, looked out at the two men standing behind him.

'Yeah, you've all had your chances. But it's too late now.' Without waiting for a response, Cal stepped back into Pug's cabin. He peered into the dark corners, wanted to see the rattler with the lethal bite and blow its head off. He spoke quietly as he dragged a blanket across the body.

'I never would o' made a miner, Pug, an' now I'm goin' to have to resort to type . . . for a while at least.'

Cal was suddenly drained of feeling but his thoughts were savage. Once Pug had made him promise not to seek retribution. He wrote down his address, wanted his family to get the stash if anything should happen to him. He said that was all that really mattered.

Cal fingered the piece of paper deep in his pocket.

'Well, Pug, I'm goin' to have to disappoint you for the

first part of that, anyway,' he muttered. He stood outside the cabin and looked along the creek towards Sego Bench, listened to the wind in the canyon. Two or three other miners from the slope had joined Elms, stood silent and troubled.

Cal walked slowly and deliberately past them, setting himself for what he intended to do. The words of Harvey Elms rang through his head. *Me an' Nate should've . . . Pug could've. . . .*

'Yeah, an' *I* could've taken care of Bunns and Frisco,' he thought bitterly.

He went on towards the town, alone. He'd already forgotten the other miners. He didn't see them look guiltily at each other, or hear what Elms said.

'What in hell's name are we waitin' for? I'll get Pug's shotgun. It'll be first light soon.'

# 19
# Off the Street

Back at the Arizona Rose, Frank Henner was shouting her name as he climbed the stairs. When the knock came, Lauren turned from the window where she'd been waiting and watching dawn break. She slowly crossed the room and opened the door. The once cow-thief, now saloon-owner came into the room. Lauren saw the anguish on his face when he turned and faced her.

'Christ, I never knew it would come to this. Time's come to hit the flats, Lauren,' he blurted out.

'One day . . . or night, you're goin' to knock on my door, Frank, an' I'll be pleased to see you. What is it now?' Lauren asked.

'That scum of Denton Lome . . . they shot Pug Edgcumbe . . . took his stash. They got him snake-bit 'til he talked. Crow knows who did it . . . him an' some miners. They'll wake this town, then take it apart lookin' for 'em. Lome's gone too far this time.'

'Cal? He's here . . . in Sego Bench?' Lauren stuttered.

'Yeah. Harvey Elms said he's gunnin' for Bunns, Gentle an' Jared Munroe. He'll take on Lome as well, if he shows.'

'Denton Lome's got backing ... too much to lose. He'll shoot Cal himself if he has to.'

'No Lauren, he'll try. I've seen Calvin Crow when he's angry ... been with him. Elms says he's got a gun now.'

Lauren walked quickly to the window.

'Where is he, Frank?' she said, her voice trembling.

Henner shrugged. 'Somewhere along the street, I guess. He ain't goin' into hidin', that's for sure. I was goin' to ask you to come to California with me, Lauren,' he continued uncertainly. 'It ain't troubled, an it's warm an' sunny ... good for your health. But in the circumstances, I'll just be wishin' you good fortune. I reckon you'll be needin' it. If you ever. . . .'

But Lauren hadn't waited for him to finish. She'd grabbed a shawl, was past him and already into the hall. She took the stairs as fast as she could, ran through the empty saloon.

In the deserted street, a fresh wind was lashing the torches that still guttered from the night before. As she looked towards the Long Lizard, a man stepped through the batwings, on to the boardwalk. Calvin Crow wasn't wearing a hat and he'd discarded his coat. In his left hand he carried the big Green River knife; in his right, the Frontier Colt he'd bought from Ellwood's Variety Store.

He waited for Lauren as she ran towards him in the street.

'Cal ... stop!' she yelled. 'They'll kill you ... they're takin' over the town.'

'You stay out of this, Lauren. No one's takin' *me* over ... *no one.* I promised Pug I'd take his money to his wife an' kids.'

But Lauren didn't want to stay out of it; she moved forward until she stood in the street below him.

'He didn't mean for you to get killed.'

'No, an' I didn't mean for *him* to get killed . . . he was my friend,' Cal said, trying to hide the hurt in his eyes. 'He ain't goin' to die alone, I'll see to that. And if you stand there much longer, *you'll* be the one to get me killed. Now get out of the street,' he snapped. 'I got some more entertainin' to do.'

'Go an' fight your stupid fight then,' she choked, tear-fully. 'Go an' die with your stupid gun an' your stupid knife.'

Cal stepped down from the boardwalk. He took a long look at Lauren, remembered what Pug had said. Then he turned his back on her, walked into the centre of the street. He quickly made it to the east end of town, stopped outside Bernie's Bar. It was where Gentle and Bunns had taken to, since the fist-fight with Cal.

He didn't have to make it loud. Most of the town knew what he wanted. His voice would cut through the ominous silence, reach the bar.

'If you're in there,' he called. 'Gentle. . . Bunns . . . Munroe. One at a time, or all together. I ain't goin' anywhere.'

Nothing happened, and Cal almost wilted from the extreme silence. He turned to look back down the street and raised his voice.

'Gentle . . . Frisco Gentle . . . lead 'em out, you cowardly son-of-a-bitch.'

The breeze caught Cal's words, whipped them along the street towards where Lauren was watching. She was standing inside the swing doors of the Arizona Rose when she saw the three men. They stepped from a cut-off alleyway and she recognized them immediately: the small, bespectacled Frisco Gentle, the big, black-suited Oaky Bunns and Jared Munroe.

The men walked slowly towards Bernie's Bar, and Lauren heard Frisco Gentle's high-pitched, sniggering response to Cal's taunt.

'The mail-order cowboy's come to say goodbye.'

But it was then that someone else called out. It was deathly and hollow sounding.

'Crow!'

Cal had seen the men in the street, turned fast to confront the new voice. From less than thirty feet, one of the doors of the bar gaped and he saw the barrel of Denton Lome's short carbine. Too late, he raised his Colt and cursed at the flash from Lome's gun. He dropped his knife as the bullets hammered him into the hard ground.

The sheriff of San Simon Territory stepped on to the boardwalk fronting the bar. Poker-faced, he extended his arm, waved the carbine down at Cal's twitching body.

# 20
# Body of Men

In the few seconds it took from seeing the men in the street, hearing Denton Lome call his name, and the gunshots, Cal lived a chilling eternity.

He was half turned when Lome's first shot thumped into his body, high in his left shoulder. His body snapped back with the impact, then his legs folded when a second bullet shattered his left thigh. The rutted dirt of the street slanted up at him, hit him like a slammed door. But on seeing Lome, something from the dark recesses of his mind had made him hold on to the Colt.

Fighting the pain, Cal tried to get back on his feet. Lome levered a shell into his gun, took a step to the edge of the boardwalk, as a new sound cut the breathy silence. It was the angry yell of Harvey Elms and the miners as they advanced from the creek end of the street.

Lome immediately wheeled to face them, his attitude harsh and threatening. He swung the carbine, raised his voice as Bunns, Gentle and Munroe took up defensive positions below him in the street.

'Turn around. You're threatenin' the law an' order of

151

the town. Get off the street, before I order my deputies to open fire.'

Harvey Elms and the small group of miners had been joined by Don Bonito and Nathan Bowler and they hardly broke step.

'Deputies, Ha! They're murderin' scum an' you're outnumbered, Sheriff,' Elms yelled back.

The men were less than fifty feet away when Cal lifted his head, saw Lome smile. He twisted the other way and saw the reason, the fearful look in the eyes of the men as they got closer. That's what Lome had seen; he knew that with a single shot he could break their doubtful bravery.

Cal gritted his teeth. Then he squeezed his eyes tight shut for an instant, forced his agonized, bleeding body into a roll. First it was his leg, then his shoulder that screamed with pain. But his right arm was free and the polished steel of the Colt gleamed bright in his hand.

'Look out!' Bunns roared, swinging a Winchester at Cal.

Cal brought his arm up and with his thumb dragged back the hammer of the Colt. He pulled the trigger at the same time as the carbine blasted, as Lome's final shot ground into the hard dirt.

Lome was a big man, strong and determined, and it took a second shot from Cal to stop him. The man's chin dropped and his eyes stared down at the crimson mash of his chest. His face went grey, his teeth grinded in agony and his carbine clattered on to the boardwalk.

In the rictus of death, the mask of Lome's authority fell away, and Cal tried to find a place for him in his memory. Their eyes met and Lome raised his arm. Then as his legs finally stopped working, he mouthed a single word. He waited until it registered with Cal, then an evil grin twisted his face and, eyes wide open, he fell to the boardwalk.

Lome's henchmen stood spellbound as Cal swore, pumped another bullet into the crumpled form of the sheriff.

There was a brief, heavy silence, and then the street echoed to the thunderous racket of the miners' concentrated gunfire. The front of the saloon became hazed with dust as bullets and scattershot blasted the clapboarded façade. The batwings splintered and wood slivers filled the air. Above Munroe's head, a glass window was shattered, the wooden frame chewed apart by the barrage of lead.

Frisco Gentle hit Nate Bowler when he fired into the advancing miners, but Cal saw him cut down immediately. A bullet hit him directly between the eyes, crushing his spectacles and caving in the front of his face. His smooth, hairless flesh disappeared in a gush of thick blood and he turned, clawed himself along on his knees until he dropped.

Bunns made the mistake of reaching for the carbine Lome had dropped. He'd only just closed his fingers over the weapon when Harvey Elms reached him. There was a short-lived scream as the man was pulled from the boardwalk, trampled under the boots of the following body of men. As soon as Macey Hume and Don Bonito lifted him back to his feet, Bonito's fist curled round and clubbed the heavy man across the jaw. Blood sprayed from Bunns's mouth and he went down again. He was still trying to get up when Hume booted him viciously in the side.

'Pug would have wanted someone to do that,' he rasped.

'Pug would've wanted him to get a lot more'n a kickin',' Elms yelled out savagely. 'Grab the bastard.'

Bunns lay staring up at the miners. His mouth hung open, bright blood oozing across his teeth and gums as they dragged him back to his feet.

In the chaos, Jared Munroe knew he had no chance, could only see one way out. He threw himself out into the street, his hands clutching for Cal's throat. But in his agonized move to shoot at Lome, Cal had regained his knife. He'd already grasped the hilt, twisted the big blade upright when Munroe landed heavily alongside him. Cal could almost smell the greasy sweat of Munroe's tortured face as he impaled himself through the heart. The man stared hopelessly for his few last croaky words.

'I'm . . . stuck . . . to . . . your . . . knife . . . Crow.'

'Yeah, well you should o' stuck to cattle-rustling,' Cal whispered, trying to blink through the lightning bolts of pain.

Somewhere above him he saw the dark shape of Oaky Bunns. He saw the dying man's staccato hop as the body twisted on the end of a short rope.

'We know who the others are,' he heard someone shout. 'We'll burn 'em out . . . hang every goddamn one of 'em.'

Then, hands were moving him, pulling at his clothing, gently touching his face as he went in and out of black madness.

Lauren held Cal under his arms, and, with Don Bonito's help, dragged him off the street, away from the miners' deadly rebellion. She bent close to him and he heard her hard breathing, closed his eyes as daylight blurred with the warm red glow of firelight.

'I've just remembered,' he groaned. 'Pug told me not to get killed on his behalf.'

# 21
# The Damages

Cal stirred sluggishly, his tortured senses unwilling to respond to anything. He felt numb and alone. He dreamed of Walker; saw his face, distant and unclear; heard him whimpering with pain, 'I'm cold. Don't let me die, Pa.'

Then there were other figures: Dillard Groff falling into the Pecos. Jeeter Krewel, gurgling his life away. The grinning, friendly face of Pug Edgcumbe coughing with delight as he missed a spit of Dark Mule.

Then Cal imagined Denton Lome standing on the boardwalk wielding his short-tooled carbine. Then a pale, ghostlike image of the tall man without the long, drooping moustaches, the underlying structure of his face mouthing the word 'Boss' at him as he lay in the street.

'Gibson. Crick Gibson,' Cal yelled and sat up.

The pain was harsh and immediate, jarred him into wakefulness. He opened and closed his eyes, got pushed back down by someone as he fought the dream.

There was a warm smell of food, and a little boy was staring down at him. Behind him was a Mexican woman who smiled. Cal recognized her as the wife of the man who ran the relay station at Lordsburg.

He made a weary smile.

'I know where I am but . . . how'd I get here? You understand me?' he asked.

'No, *señor*, I never understand men. But yes, I can use your language,' the woman replied. 'It was the lady, Miss Lauren . . . she brought you.'

Cal looked closely at the boy, closed his eyes again.

'How long? How long have I been here?' he asked.

'Two days . . . two nights.' The woman tapped the boy with her foot. 'Go tell the lady,' she said, indicating for him to move away from Cal's bedside.

Cal tried to raise himself, swore and let his head fall back.

'That's it, *señor*, let them come to you.' The woman shook her head and turned away.

Cal lay still. He could smell the damage to his body, the carbolic soap. He felt the warm hurt and he thought of Denton Lome whose bullets had torn into him. Then he remembered Barkdale penitentiary, the carbine in the hands of Crick Gibson.

He was shivering, suffering from the ordeal, when he heard the door open. He waited for the woman to say something, but she didn't and he opened his eyes. Lauren Garth was holding a bowl of soup, and she smiled.

'I guess you ain't performin' tonight,' he said, looking at her dirty hands, soot-smudged face and clothing.

She shook her head, spoke quietly.

'No Cal, there's not much to sing about. The Arizona Rose has been burned down, along with every other saloon. They started while you were still lyin' in the street. Right now, there ain't much left standin' in Sego Bench.'

'The miners did that?' Cal asked.

'Yeah. They discovered Lome was runnin' just about every business in town. They brought in Hamey Barge an' strung him up with three others. They took a wagon to the roarin' camp, then sent it into the Chiricahuas. I don't know what . . .' Lauren's voice trembled, broke with emotion. 'Frank said they'd take Sego Bench apart lookin' for Lome's scum. He underestimated 'em.'

Lauren was about to feed Cal the soup she'd brought in, when someone rapped impatiently on the door and entered.

'Come on in,' Cal said, irritatedly. 'It is a relay station, not a goddamn hospital.'

Harvey Elms's face was tired, his eyes sunken and dark. He nodded at Cal, looked at Lauren.

'I'm real sorry about what happened in Sego Bench, Miss Lauren,' he said. 'The agency made a rule. We treated it same as hog cholera . . . no exceptions.' He shrugged, then threw a doubtful glance at Cal. 'The stage'll be here some time after noon,' he continued. 'Frank Henner'll be on it.'

Elms laid the beaver knife beside Cal.

'If you need anything, just say the word. We're grateful for what you did.' He nodded and went out with the Mexican woman, closing the door behind them.

Cal stared at his knife.

'What's that about Henner? You got somethin' goin'?' he asked warily.

'No. He thought we had . . . wanted to, that's all.'

158

'So why's he leavin'?'

'I think he wanted that to be private. He wrote you a letter, asked me to give it to you. Then he changed his mind and wanted it back.'

Cal made a gruff, frustrated sound.

'What the hell's it got to do with me . . . this letter?'

'If I tell you what it said, promise me you'll drink this soup.'

'Yeah, I promise. I ain't had a letter before. Even one I don't get to get.'

'Frank said he didn't want you on his tail . . . said there was a lot you didn't know. It wasn't a long letter.'

'Just tell me, Lauren.'

'He wrote: 'That time out on the rail line over the Pecos. One o' those men who was with me was there to meet Dillard Groff. And the man you killed at Las Cruces – Jeeter Krewel – we'd become partners. It was going to be the four of us. Then there was that one on the coach – the one you took his arm off – he was in on it too.' I can't remember it *all* exact, but I think that was their names,' Lauren said.

'Yeah, you got their names right. Is that all?' Cal asked wearily.

'No. There was a bit more. It was: "People don't seem to live long when you're around. But now you've won . . . don't need to go wieldin' that big knife any more".'

Lauren stopped talking, and Cal opened his eyes.

'What else?'

'He said he was headin' back East. That was about it.'

'About it?'

'He said you couldn't make his life any worse. Then there was some personal stuff.' Lauren sighed unhappily.

'It seems there's a lot folk don't know, an' most of it fixes around you.'

Cal made tired noises.

'What do *you* think, Lauren?' he asked her gently.

'Frank said you were a man full of hate. That's why he wrote that letter. I think he just wanted *me* to see it.'

'No, Lauren,' Cal heaved himself up a bit. 'He wrote that letter because he thought I'd find out about him . . . wonder where he fitted in. An' he won't hear me shout "guilty" if he ain't here.'

'You're a strange man, Calvin Crow,' Lauren said, giving him a long, searching look. 'It's almost noon. Maybe I should take the stage,' she added without much conviction.

Cal reached out a hand, pushed the knife to the floor.

'Don't go, Lauren. Stay here . . . feed me some o' that bean soup. I ain't wieldin' the big knife any more, look.'